16355

What readers think

This book is jam pac~~ked~~ ~~3 FEB 2018~~
You never quite know wha~~t~~ ...
Liam Clifton (age 10)

Danny Bouygues travels through places you can't imagine because they're so diabolically abysmal. Although this may seem like a miserable story, never fear for this book is not all snivel! It has such a gripping storyline I could hardly put it down. This book is exceedingly outstanding and hilarious. *Pranaav Vijayan (age 10)*

Brilliant description, especially of the skeleton army. My favourite character is King Bones because he is funny and a caring soul. Well, if skeletons have souls. I think Chris Hallatt Wells will have to write a second story because of the wonderful mysterious ending. *James McConnel (age 10)*

Fantastic. My only criticism is that, for all this enjoyment, the book isn't longer. Did I mention it was irresistibly funny? *Finn (age 11)*

Older readers...

A rollicking, hilarious, page-turning romp. Chris Hallatt Wells understands what keeps children gripped and writes with wit, originality, energy and fun. Beautifully irreverently written with energy, originality fun and style . The characters burst from the page, the gleeful prose glitters, the plot never lets up the pace. *Helen Fielding, Bridget Jones's Diary.*

King Bones is a story packed ~~with~~ ... ion that spreads through its pages ... certain to ignite any reader's ima ... *...eth P Jones, The Thornthwaite Inhe...*

D1464422

KING BONES

CHRIS HALLATT WELLS

Published in the UK by Everything with Words Limited 3rd Floor,
Premier House, 12-13 Hatton Garden, London EC1N 8AN
www.everythingwithwords.com

Text copyright © Chris Hallatt Wells 2017

Illustrations © Steph von Reiswitz 2017

Printed and bound in Great Britain by Clays Ltd, St Ives plc

A CIP catalogue record for this book is available
from the British Library.

ISBN 978-1-911427-04-9

Lucille, thank you for your support and encouraging kicks (verbal). I needed both. And Spencer for demanding a story about skeletons. Lily, you'll have to wait for a mention until the next book.

Chapter 1

THE UNUSUAL SUSPECTS

DANNY BOUYGUES WAS probably the happiest child in England, until the night his parents were arrested for breaking into the Tower of London and stealing the Crown Jewels.

It was the most spectacular crime in history. First, the thieves crossed the wide grassy moat. Then they scaled the high battlements, eluding dozens of infrared security cameras and laser motion detectors. Silently, they sneaked past the medieval Beefeaters and the modern soldiers armed with the latest machine guns. Undetected, the thieves broke into the Jewel House and defeated the best burglar alarm ever invented. Somehow they opened the massive bombproof steel door to the vault and, once inside they sliced through the inches thick unbreakable glass to reach the priceless treasures within.

The thieves stole everything. Everything! The gold and platinum crowns encrusted with diamonds and rubies and emeralds and sapphires, some the size of swans' eggs. The golden orbs, the swords and spurs, the sceptres, the sacred spoons, the royal armills and Her Majesty's favourite garters.

The Queen was not amused.

Carrying their precious plunder, the thieves left as stealthily as they had come. They closed and locked the vault, re-crossed battlements and the moat, and vanished into the London night.

The police were completely clueless. Only a handful of the world's greatest super-thieves were brave *and* clever enough to carry out the daring midnight raid. But all the usual suspects were either in prison or in hospital or dead. And the prime suspect was all three at the same time. A few months earlier, Barry *'Ice Pick'* McSweeny's reckless plan to steal the lions from London Zoo had gone tragically wrong. The lions did not want to be stolen and they ate most of him. The bits of Ice Pick the lions did not swallow were sent to Wormwood Scrubs prison, where they survived just long enough to expire on the very night of the Crown Jewels burglary. The police were tempted to question him anyway, but they knew it was a waste of time. Ice Pick came from an infamous family of London crooks who had robbed and murdered since the first Queen Elizabeth was on the throne. And no McSweeny – alive or dead – would dream of helping the police with their enquiries.

Which left the unusual suspects. And none were more unusual than Mr and Mrs Bouygues.

No one suspected Danny's parents because it was impossible to imagine two people less likely to be the world's greatest super thieves.

The Bouygues – it is pronounced *'Bweeg'*, although most people said *'Boo-Geez'* or even *'Bogey'* – lived in a rose-covered cottage near the perfect English village where they ran the village restaurant, which was probably the most spectacularly unsuccessful restaurant in the history of restaurants.

The problem was Mr Bouygues' cooking.

It was too good.

Much too good.

Because Mr Bouygues was, without any shadow of doubt, the greatest chef ever to wield a wooden spoon. Especially a wooden spoon that he had carved himself from a broken toilet seat. Mr Bouygues liked to reuse and recycle. 'Waste not want not' was Mr Bouygues' motto. Well, *one* of his mottos.

Mr Bouygues was a wizard in the kitchen. He was so amazing he created stupendous feasts using ingredients other chefs threw away. Like rotten carrots turning to orange mush and raw potato peelings (preferably black and slimy) and withered apples hollowed out by wasps and tubs of margarine sprouting green and purple fungus.

And when he used fresh vegetables, Mr Bouygues always chose the ones that were crawling with bugs.

'Why?' Danny had asked one lunchtime as he was watching a fat lime green caterpillar munching on his cabbage. Across the plate, a herd of baby slugs were hard at work on Danny's broccoli.

'Because butterflies know their veg,' replied Mr Bouygues, patiently.

Patiently because Mr Bouygues was always patient. Unlike most other parents, Mr Bouygues had never smacked Danny, not once. And he did not shout either, or scream, or threaten dire punishments, no matter how dreadful the thing was that he had just caught Danny doing. Not even when he caught Danny lighting a large bonfire in his bedroom. Even then Mr Bouygues did not explode like any normal parent would. Oh no.

Patiently, Mr Bouygues explained why lighting a bonfire in your bedroom was not the most sensible way to toast marshmallows, even if you had opened the window to let the smoke escape. Then, patiently, Mr Bouygues helped carry the logs and kindling and the cans of petrol downstairs and into the back garden. And there – at a safe distance from the house – Mr Bouygues patiently taught Danny how to build a variety of different types of bonfires suitable for every camping situation: the classic teepee bonfire, which is the ideal fire to sit around telling stories; a pit fire when it was too windy for a teepee; and the right sort of fire when you are lost in a Siberian forest in midwinter and the mercury's frozen solid in the thermometer and your breath turns to ice crystals that flutter to the ground with a soft tinkle.

Basically, it was burning a whole tree.

And lastly, in case Danny should ever need to camp in a swamp, Mr Bouygues showed him how to construct a log raft held together with knotted reeds, cover the raft in packed earth and build the fire on that.

'...so they only lay their eggs on the tastiest cabbages and string beans,' continued Mr Bouygues, patiently. 'Now eat up quick or he'll have your Brussels sprouts too!'

Danny waited until Mr Bouygues' back was turned and rolled his sprouts towards the hungry caterpillar.

The meat Mr Bouygues used in his cooking was even more disgusting than his vegetables. Mr Bouygues did not believe in buying meat from supermarkets, pre-sliced and bloodless, laid in a white polystyrene coffin and wrapped in cellophane.

'Meat should look like it's come from an animal,' said Mr Bouygues. 'With blood and fur and legs and claws and teeth.'

He did not like butchers' shops either. 'Nasty antiseptic places,' said Mr Bouygues with a shiver. 'They remind me of hospitals.'

So where did Mr Bouygues get his meat?

From the motorway.

It was a daily ritual for Mr Bouygues. Every morning before the sun had risen (he had to start early to beat the crows) Mr Bouygues set forth on his bicycle to scour the local roads and motorways for fox and hedgehog pancakes. He scraped the pancakes off the tarmac with a spade and brought them home in a tin bucket swinging from the handlebars of his bicycle.

If the pancakes had been dead for a while – pounded flat by passing lorries and cars, and baked iron-hard in the sun – Mr Bouygues filled the bucket with pond water to soften the meat.

'Never tap water,' Mr Bouygues explained, patiently, as he knelt beside the village pond filling his tin bucket with murky liquid wriggling with leeches and water beetles and dragonfly larvae, and filthy with blue-green algae and duck poo. 'There are too many chemicals in tap water and they spoil the flavour.'

Swarms of insects found their way into Mr Bouygues' kitchen too. Cockroaches, of course, and woodlice, ladybirds, wasps, horse-flies, houseflies, bluebottles, hornets, gnats, moths and spiders. Although, strictly speaking, spiders are 'arachnids', not insects, and woodlice are 'crustaceans' like prawns and lobsters, so they're not really bugs at all. They are just smaller and less fashionable than their ocean-dwelling cousins. And harder to peel.

It did not matter what species of creature they were

because Mr Bouygues had a recipe for anything that crept or crawled or buzzed or stung.

Even dung beetles. Mr Bouygues was especially fond of dung beetles. Luckily, there was a dairy farm next door to the Bouygues' cottage, so there was never a shortage of fresh, steaming cow pats and the beetles that feasted upon them.

By all the laws of nature, hygiene and French haute cuisine, Mr Bouygues' food should have been disgusting. Yet, somehow, in Mr Bouygues' magical hands these vile and putrid and frequently downright poisonous ingredients were turned into dishes fit for The Queen. Mr Bouygues' food tasted absolutely delicious. His starters were stupendous! His main courses, magnificent! And his puddings were superlative!

Unfortunately, when written on the restaurant menu they sounded absolutely disgusting.

Nobody wants to eat road-kill hedgehog pancakes rehydrated in duck-poop pond water fizzing with insect larvae, served with a dollop of rotten carrot mush and a salad of black and slimy potato peelings, with a side dish of crispy caterpillars self-stuffed with cabbage and wok-fried in purple margarine.

And for pudding they definitely don't want to eat dung beetle ice cream with centipede and millipede sprinkles. Which was a shame. Dung beetle ice cream was Danny's favourite. It was a taste sensation and deliciously crunchy too.

So almost no one came to the Bouygues' restaurant and absolutely no one came twice. So the Bouygues were spectacularly poor. They did not seem to mind though and the Bouygues were never less than extremely happy.

Mrs Bouygues was French. *Bouygues* is a French name and

it was her name before it was Mr Bouygues'. Mr Bouygues was born a *Gruntfuttock*. When they married, *Mademoiselle* Bouygues refused to become *Madame* Gruntfuttock. And who can blame her? Instead Mr Gruntfuttock became *Monsieur* Bouygues. Danny was glad they had done it that way round. It was better to be called '*Bogey*' occasionally than '*Gruntfuttock*' always.

Strangely – and this is very odd – despite being entirely French, Mrs Bouygues was completely useless in the kitchen. She could not make a jam sandwich without it going horribly wrong. And when she tried something more adventurous – like a baked potato – she was positively dangerous. The spud was sure to explode or implode or catch fire or sometimes all three at the same time. Which was interesting to watch, but less so when Danny was starving hungry after a long day at school.

A traditional French breakfast with all the trimmings was the only meal Mrs Bouygues could make safely. Mrs Bouygues had one *every* morning. The breakfast part was a strong black coffee, thick and dark as Jamaican treacle and bitter as road tar. The 'trimmings' was an even stronger cigarette that smelled like the cow dung in the field next door.

But nobody cared about her dreadful cooking because Mrs Bouygues more than made up for every kitchen calamity by being irresistibly lovely and smelling of croissants hot from the oven. Croissants baked by Mr Bouygues. Mrs Bouygues' croissants smelled like burning car tyres and tasted even worse.

Chapter 2

THE ARREST

THE POLICE CAME in the night.

It was an ordinary Wednesday in an ordinary week towards the end of a perfectly ordinary month. Ordinary for Danny and his parents, that is. It had been an extraordinary month for the police. Every policeman and woman and horse and dog in England had been searching for the Crown Jewels. Every other investigation was cancelled.

On that ordinary Wednesday night, before he went to bed, Danny fed the goats and the rabbits-that-weren't-pets and locked the chickens into the hen house. He said *'bon nuit'* to his mother, *'goodnight'* to his father and fell asleep listening to the frustrated screams of the local foxes as they tried to break into the Bouygues' hen house to murder the chickens. The foxes tried to murder the Bouygues' chickens most nights. Usually they failed, but not always. The dreadful din would have driven most children insane. Except Danny Bouygues had grown up with it and for him the noise was as sweet as a lullaby sung by angels. When the foxes were off murdering someone else's chickens Danny did not sleep a wink.

It happened on the last stroke of midnight.

Without warning, the police smashed through the front door of the Bouygues' cottage, blasting the wood to splinters with an iron battering ram. The police were dressed entirely in black. Black helmets, body armour and steel-toed boots protected their bodies. Black masks and goggles hid their faces. Even their machine guns were black. The only colour was the red beam of their laser sights.

The armed police stormed through the cottage shouting and breaking things. They found Mr Bouygues asleep in bed and threw him onto the floor and chained his wrists behind his back, pulling the handcuffs tight until Mr Bouygues gasped in pain.

Mrs Bouygues was too quick to be caught in bed. The same instance the police smashed through her front door, Mrs Bouygues was wide awake. A heartbeat later she leapt through the bedroom window, diving headfirst and shattering the glass. She tumbled in the air three times and landed on her feet, crouched like a cat in Mr Bouygues' herb garden, amongst his stinging nettles and dandelions and the falling shards of glass.

But there was no escape that way. The police had the cottage surrounded.

They found Mrs Bouygues in the hen house hiding with the chickens. She had a smear of bird dung on her cheek and strands of hay in her chestnut-coloured hair. Splinters of broken glass sparkled like fine diamonds on her nightie. It was Mrs Bouygues' favourite nightie: luxurious silk the colour of ripe plums. It was a present from Mr Bouygues.

Mrs Bouygues was far too lovely to be considered dangerous, so when she promised to behave the police agreed to leave her wrists uncuffed.

That was their first mistake.

The second was leaving the youngest and least experienced

policeman to guard the lovely prisoner, whilst the other officers searched the cottage. The young policeman was so young he had not started shaving and his face was still covered in pimples. He had never kissed a girl either, not once. He was too shy to ask in case they said 'no' because of his spots.

The third mistake was the young policeman's. It was the last mistake he ever made.

It was a chill and frosty night. When the young policeman heard his prisoner's teeth chattering – Mrs Bouygues was still only wearing her nightie – being a kind fellow, he took off his black policeman's jacket and put it around Mrs Bouygues' shoulders to keep her warm.

'*Merci Monsieur Flic,*' whispered Mrs Bouygues and she pecked the policeman gently on the cheek.

His first kiss! The young policeman's pimply, unrazored face blushed the same colour as Mrs Bouygues' nightie.

Then he remembered his gun! It was in his jacket pocket.

Except it was not, not any more. Mrs Bouygues had felt the shape against her leg and, in a movement too quick to see, the gun was in her hand.

She pressed the black metal barrel against the young policeman's chest. Only the thickness of his cotton shirt and thermal vest lay between him and certain death. His cheeks turned from hot plum jam to cold banana custard.

Mrs Bouygues' bright eyes darted left and right. The coast was clear. The other police officers were either inside the house or talking self-importantly into their radios and boasting of their success, or secretly phoning the newspapers to sell the story. No one was looking in Mrs Bouygues' direction. She could walk away and vanish without a trace.

It crossed her mind. The young policeman saw it written on her face. Half of him wished that she would. Then the moment passed and the steel in Mrs Bouygues' eyes melted to caramel. As much as she longed to escape, Mrs Bouygues was French, which meant she was far too honourable to take advantage of his kindness. Slyly, so the other officers would not notice, Mrs Bouygues slipped the gun into the young policeman's hand, with a wink and a smile so he would know it was their secret.

Meanwhile the Bouygues' cottage was being torn to pieces. The police slashed the mattresses and sofas with knives and pulled out the stuffing. They ripped up the floorboards and broke holes in the walls and ceilings. They tore pages from books and smashed ornaments. With crowbars they heaved up the ancient flagstones from the kitchen floor and dug holes in the brown earth beneath – earth that had not been disturbed for six hundred years. They even sent the smallest policeman crawling up the chimney with a torch strapped to his head.

Danny's bedroom was the last place they looked. A woman police inspector gripped Danny's arm as her officers searched the room with the same indelicate thoroughness. They were about to give up when the smallest policeman crawled beneath Danny's bed and found the Crown Jewels of England cunningly concealed in a large cardboard box that had once contained Saint Lucian bananas.

Through his bedroom window Danny watched his parents climb into a waiting van. The dark night was turned blue by the flashing lights of a hundred police cars.

Chapter 3

FALSE CONFESSIONS

THE BOUYGUES CONFESSED to their crime immediately, but the police refused to believe them. It was impossible! Ridiculous!

Mrs Bouygues was far too lovely to be a thief and the thought of sending her to prison made her interrogators feel sick. So they ignored her confession and changed the subject from burglary to Mrs Bouygues' childhood in France. They had endless questions about that. About her growing up barefoot in the vineyards of *Gascoigne* and her holidays in *Cap d'Antibes* on the French Riviera.

Which had nothing to do with the Crown Jewels investigation and everything to do with Mrs Bouygues' French accent. Quite simply, the police officers had fallen in love with the way she said *'Gascoigne'* and the image of Mrs Bouygues holidaying in *Cap d'Antibes*.

Especially with the image of her holidaying in *Cap d'Antibes*.

It was different with Mr Bouygues. It could not have been more different. The police *wanted* to believe that Mr Bouygues was guilty because they hated him with a passion that verged on madness. Not for being a crook. The police are connoisseurs of fine crime and the Crown Jewels robbery was the greatest robbery in history. Which meant Mr Bouygues was the greatest thief in history. Which meant the police officers who caught him were the greatest detectives in history. Which should have made them rather fond of Mr Bouygues or at least grateful.

What, then, was the reason for their hatred?

It was jealousy. Pure 100 percent undiluted ugly jealousy.

Partly because Mr Bouygues lived a life of free adventure, without concern for money or possessions or any of the countless worries that squeeze the happiness from other adults.

The police were jealous about the chickens too, and the rabbits. Until they discovered that the rabbits were not pets. When Mr Bouygues told them that the rabbits were for eating, the police hated Mr Bouygues even more, although the rabbits belonged to Mrs Bouygues and Mr Bouygues would never dream of cooking a fresh bunny.

The rose-covered cottage did not help either. The police were very bitter about that because they lived in ugly cities in pokey flats or tiny houses with tinier gardens.

But mostly they hated Mr Bouygues for being married to Mrs Bouygues, because compared to Mrs Bouygues their own wives seemed plain and dull, and their lives were empty and pointless.

Their hatred of Mr Bouygues had no limit. They hated him as much as one human being can hate another living thing.

Until the day Mr Bouygues took charge of the cooking in the canteen of Scotland Yard.

It was a transformation. From their first taste of Mr Bouygues' *haricot au sauce tomate sur pain grille avec fromage* which roughly translates as baked beans on toast with cheese, the police fell under a spell that was differently, but equally, hypnotic to that woven by Mrs Bouygues' Gallic smile.

After their second helping of frogspawn & cockroach porridge, the police knew they had to let the Bouygues go free. Even if the Bouygues were guilty as hell, sending them to prison was an infinitely worse crime than pinching a few gaudy baubles and bits of greasy yellow metal.

A taxi was called to take the prisoners home, when the police collided with an unexpected problem. The Bouygues refused to withdraw their confessions.

The police begged and pleaded, but the Bouygues would not listen to reason. So the police had no choice. If the Bouygues would not save themselves, the police would have to do it for them, and they started inventing excuses for disbelieving the Bouygues' confessions.

Motive was the first excuse. The Bouygues did not have one. The Bouygues were happy to tell the police everything else: how they broke into the Tower of London; how they scaled the wall; how they had disabled the burglar alarm; and how they escaped (on a tandem bicycle carrying the Crown Jewels in a tin bucket swinging from the handlebars. Mrs Bouygues gave the impression that she had done most of the peddling because all French people think they are brilliant in the saddle. The truth was very different. It is a long time since a Frenchie won the Tour du France and Mr Bouygues was by far the stronger cyclist. Mrs Bouygues was little more than a beautiful passenger).

But they refused to say *why* they did it.

Then there was the mystery of the missing diamond. The police counted 23,577 jewels glittering on the treasures they found under Danny's bed. But there was no trace of the 23,578th. And that most precious treasure of all: the *Koh-i-Noor*.

The Koh-i-Noor was an orb of sparkling rock the size of a child's fist. It was the most fabulous pebble in history, worth more than the rest of the Crown Jewels put together. It was worth more than many countries because, according to ancient legend, whoever owns the Koh-i-Noor will rule the world and for that reason, for thousands of years, the bloodiest wars had been fought to possess it.

The Koh-i-Noor should have been glued with gold into the Queen's favourite crown, the one she wore on birthdays and special occasions. But the golden glue was broken and where the diamond used to be there was a gaping hole.

The Bouygues admitted removing the Koh-i-Noor and hiding it, but they refused to say where. Which did not make any sense. The diamond was of no use to the Bouygues in prison and if they gave it up the police could pretend the robbery had never happened. They could blame the cleaners of the Tower of London for accidentally sweeping up the treasures, which somehow ended up in a banana box under a child's bed in a rose-covered cottage.

'*Non,*' said Mrs Bouygues, shaking her head, sending glossy ropes of chestnut curls tumbling across her beautiful face. '*Arlzo eet breks m'art zat eye kaynut tail ewe.*'

A brutal police sergeant, who had the face of a heavyweight boxer who had lost most of his fights, burst into sobs. The sergeant was particularly in love with Mrs Bouygues.

'Sorry,' said Mr Bouygues, putting a consoling arm around the sergeant's heaving shoulders. 'Would you like a mini Scotch egg?'

Mr Bouygues had cooked the conker-sized and coloured snacks on the radiator in his cell, using minced mouse meat and pigeon eggs collected from the roof of Scotland Yard (which was why the snacks were so small), and, in place of breadcrumbs, dried cockroaches crushed with the heel of his shoe.

Mr Bouygues' Scotch eggs were delicious beyond description. Far too delicious to be made by the hands of a master criminal. Which was when the police began to suspect that Danny Bouygues might be the real thief. It made perfect sense. After all, the Crown Jewels had been found under Danny's bed.

Suddenly everything fell into place. The Bouygues couldn't tell the police about their motive because they didn't have one! And they didn't have a motive because they didn't commit the crime! And they couldn't say where the Koh-i-Noor was hidden because they hadn't pinched it!

Eureka! The police officers cheered and slapped each other on the back, spilling their beer (the Bouygues' interrogators had moved to the snug bar of the Pig & Whistle pub to invent their excuses; in Scotland Yard there were too many hidden microphones and nosey lawyers). How could they have been so stupid, they laughed, when the truth was blindingly obvious? The Bouygues were covering up for their horrible son. They were trying to protect Danny by taking the blame for his horrendous crime!

It was the sort of thing any parent would do to save their child.

Which made the police love the Bouygues even more.

And like Danny even less.

Chapter 4

CRIME AND PUNISHMENT

THE LADY IN the green coat refused to say where she was taking Danny. She did not answer any of his questions. She would not even look at him.

Danny was not surprised, not any more. In the weeks since his parents' arrest, Danny's life had changed beyond all recognition. Everyone he met had been cruel without exception: the police who guarded his cell; the woman who brought his meals; the detectives who interrogated him; and the lawyer who was meant to protect him. The lawyer was the worst of the lot; she plotted with the police to find Danny guilty.

The detectives had questioned Danny non-stop for days, trying to break him and make him confess to the crime. They took turns shouting until their faces swelled and veins bulged and throbbed on their foreheads.

How had he broken into the Tower?

How did he switch off the alarm?

How did he escape?

And where was the Koh-i-Noor!

The police asked the same questions a thousand times. But Danny did not crack, not once. He stuck to his story, never changing the tiniest detail.

'It's a mistake,' Danny told them. 'I've never been to the

Tower of London. And I've definitely never broken into it or stolen the Crown Jewels. Someone else must have hidden them under my bed.'

But he didn't know who or how or when or why.

When the police asked him about the missing diamond, Danny swore he had never heard of the Koh-i-Noor and he had not the faintest idea where it might be hidden.

His answers made the detectives smoke. Danny's lawyer shook her head in disgust at Danny's repeated lies and, under the table, she pinched his leg with her sharp nails. And the police pretended not to notice.

Questions, questions, endless questions. But when Danny asked something – could he see his parents? Who was milking the goats? And who was feeding the chickens and the rabbits-that-weren't-pets? – no one answered. His interrogators just scowled and cracked their knuckles.

Because they knew that Danny was guilty, but they could not prove that he was lying. Which put the police in a very difficult position because they could not prove that Mr and Mrs Bouygues were lying either.

And the police had run out of time.

The English newspapers were screaming for a conviction. Every morning, front-page headlines incited anger against the Bouygues and all things French (as far as the newspapers were concerned when he changed his name from '*Gruntfuttock*' to '*Bouygues*' Danny's father had become as foreign as his wife). The headlines were so successful supermarkets were forced to remove French cheese from the fridges and replace *pain au chocolat* with hot cross buns although Easter was long past. Bottles of French wine were smashed in the streets, until the gutters of Bradford and Bristol ran red with fruity Beaujolais. Throughout England effigies of the Bouygues were burned at the stake, with ropes of onions tied around their necks and berets on their heads. The whole country stank of burning onions from Land's End to John O'Groats.

And, in London, large crowds gathered outside Scotland Yard demanding mob justice.

Excited by the hysterical reaction their lies had provoked, the newspapers began campaigning for a public execution. They even printed fake pictures of the Prince of Wales splitting logs with an axe in the gardens of Buckingham Palace and hinted that he was practising to do the job himself.

The police had to blame someone quickly before the mob stormed Scotland Yard or the Prince of Wales hurt his back. And the Bouygues were the only suspects they had. The police knew the Bouygues were innocent and Danny was guilty, but they had no choice.

Danny had watched the trial on live television.

His parents had stood side by side in the dock of the wood-panelled Courtroom Number One in the Old Bailey. As the newspapers never tired of re-telling, the Old Bailey was built on the bones of an ancient gaol. From that unhappy place, untold thousands of thieves and murderers and traitors had been taken forth to be hung or burned or boiled. The really unlucky ones had been hung and burned, and then boiled.

An ugly crowd filled the public gallery of Courtroom Number One. When they heard the jury's guilty verdict, they cheered and hooted and clapped their hands and stamped their feet with joy.

'Order! Order!' bellowed the white-wigged red-robed judge. 'I shall have order or I'll clear this court!' The judge pounded his gavel on the oak bench until the wood cracked and his wig slipped.

A tense silence descended.

The judge straightened his wig and cleared his throat and read out his sentence.

'Life imprisonment, without any possibility of parole.'

The crowd erupted with fury. Prison was not enough! The newspapers had promised them an execution! They wanted blood!

'Guards!' screamed the judge, shrieking to be heard above the riot. 'Take the prisoners down and may God have mercy on their souls!'

TV cameras zoomed in to catch the Bouygues' reactions to their life sentence. Mr Bouygues' handsome face was ashen. He gulped and wobbled and seemed about to faint. Then he recovered his composure and squeezed his wife's hand. Mrs Bouygues stared straight ahead, untouched by the judge's words or the chaos in the courtroom and the fighting mob. She had never looked more beautiful.

It was the only time Danny had seen them since the night of their arrest.

The day after the trial the lady in the green coat collected Danny from Scotland Yard and drove him away in her car.

For three hours they sped along dreary motorways past Coventry and Stoke-on-Trent. North of Manchester they left the motorway and turned due east. For another hour they travelled along roads that grew ever smaller and through towns that grew dirtier and more miserable. Until they reached Greezy, the dirtiest, the ugliest and the most miserable town in the whole of England.

And the smelliest.

There were two factories in Greezy. Grimm's Dog Food Factory and, at the other end of town, Slugg's Cat Food Factory. Depending which way the breeze was blowing, Greezy stank of putrid meat or rotting fish. When there was no wind it stank of both. And on the day Danny arrived there was not a breath of wind to stir the stink.

A graveyard was squeezed between the two factories. It was an untidy place. The tombstones were yellowed with lichen, blackened with coal soot and browned with the reeking filth that belched from the factory chimneys. The tombstones were packed tight and leaned at crazy angles almost touching, and in the narrow spaces in between, tall weeds sprouted. And somewhere inside the graveyard, hidden in the maze of tombstones, Danny could hear the sound of digging.

Shuck! as the sharp spade cut into the heavy soil.

Thunk! when the earth landed in a wheelbarrow.

Shuck!

Thunk!

Shuck!

Thunk!

The noise seemed to shake the car.

The lady in the green coat parked opposite a main entrance to the graveyard, and beside the ugliest and dirtiest house in Greezy, which made it the ugliest and dirtiest house in the whole of England and probably the entire world. The house was tall and crooked, and the roof sagged. The brick walls were speckled with wet brown scabs of condensed factory filth. The same filth had stained the windows a smeary orange.

'Where are we?' Danny asked.

The lady in the green coat snorted. She got out of her car and locked the doors in case Danny tried to escape. She dropped the car keys in her large handbag, smoothed the wrinkles from her smart coat and marched up the short garden path to the hideous house.

She rang the doorbell, pressing the button hard. Inside the hideous house an electric bell rang feebly, its sound muffled by the thick layers of moist brown scabs.

Keeping the button firmly pressed, the lady in the green coat counted down from twenty.

'19, 18, 17...'

When she reached 10 she began to tap her foot on the doorstep.

'...9, 8, 7, 6...'

Her anger mounted.

'...4, 3, 2, 1. Zero!'

'Where the hell is she!' cursed the woman and she stepped back to peer through the orange-stained windows, searching for a sign of life.

But there was none. The house was still as death.

The lady in the green coat rang the doorbell a second time, pressing even harder and forcing the button into the wall.

She began to hammer the brass doorknocker. *Tak-tak-tak-tak-tak!*

Nothing stirred.

'Damn you!' screamed the lady in the green coat and she hit the door with her balled fist, making it rattle in its frame and dislodging scabs of filth revealing spots of the gangrene-coloured paint beneath.

Again the lady in the green coat peered through the orange-stained glass. And again there was nothing to be seen or any sound to be heard, except the steady Shuck! and Thunk! that echoed from the graveyard across the road.

The lady in the green coat turned and glared at Danny.

It was a nasty vicious glare because the lady in the green coat was a nasty vicious woman. Very nasty indeed. Grown men had wilted before that stare. Women had fainted. Children cried and suffered nightmares. And this was the worst glare she had ever given because the lady in the green coat blamed Danny for keeping her waiting on the doorstep of the worst house in the worst town in England. The foul air was making her eyes sting and her lungs wheeze and it was already staining her coat orange.

The lady in the green coat meant to scare Danny to the marrow of his bones, but her glare did not have quite the effect she intended.

Instead of fainting or crying, the corners of Danny's mouth twitched. An involuntary smile creased his face. It was the first time Danny had seen the whole of the lady in the green coat's face. When she was driving he had only seen a partial reflection in the rear view mirror, mainly her eyes. Now Danny could see her whole face, it reminded him of something funny. But what?

Then Danny remembered. It was something his mother had said in the Bouygues' restaurant a few months before the arrest. Danny was working in the kitchen peeling woodlice – a tricky task requiring a powerful magnifying glass, tweezers and a steady hand – when he heard a customer screaming at Mrs Bouygues. There was nothing usual about that. Mrs Bouygues was the waitress who served the food, so she was the person that customers shouted at when they discovered what they had been eating. This customer thought she was eating Japanese udon noodles. It was an easy mistake to make. Mr Bouygues' peeled rats' tails poached in toad slime were almost identical to Japanese noodles. The main difference was the crunch; noodles do not have bones.

When Danny heard the door slam and the sound of breaking glass, he dashed into the restaurant and found his mother already cleaning up the mess.

'*Eez nerthing,*' said Mrs Bouygues and she shrugged her Gallic shrug and carried on sweeping. Mrs Bouygues had lived in England for years, so she was used to squeamish English people complaining about Mr Bouygues' food. The French are much more sensible. If it tastes nice and is not dangerously poisonous, the French will gobble up practically anything. Mr Bouygues' peeled rats' tails were poached to perfection. They were so delicious the shouty customer had eaten three bowls. She was ordering a fourth when she made the mistake of asking for the recipe.

Danny did not see the shouty customer, but he had never forgotten his mother's description.

'She had a face like a slapped bum,' Mrs Bouygues had said. Except Mrs Bouygues said '*fazz*' instead of '*face*', '*lak*' instead of '*like*', '*slept*' not '*slapped*' and '*berm*' instead of '*bum*'.

The description stuck in Danny's brain and when he looked at the lady in the green coat that is what he saw: a swollen, blotchy, red-cheeked berm wearing a blonde wig and smudgy lipstick, with four chins and whiskers poking through her makeup.

To Danny the lady in the green coat was not in the least bit scary. She was a silly bum-faced woman having a temper tantrum.

The smile turned into a giggle.

Stop it, Danny told himself. If she sees you laughing at her she'll explode.

Oh dear. The vision of the bum-faced woman exploding was the absolute worst thing Danny could have imagined. BOOM! SPLAT! And a blonde wig fluttering down from the sky to land on the singed remains of her green coat.

Danny began to choke. Another second and he would lose control.

You *have* to stop staring at her, Danny told himself and he dragged his eyes away from the lady in the green coat to look through the front window of the car.

What he saw killed Danny's giggles, instantly.

It was the people walking up and down the street. There was something odd about them. Odd and creepy. Everyone looked the same. Not identical, but similar. Very similar. They had lumpy bodies and stumpy legs and podgy, unhealthy faces. Their skin was pale as candle wax, their hair was greasy and copper-coloured, and at least half of them were cross-eyed.

It's like they're all cousins or the cousins of cousins, thought Danny.

Which was exactly what they were. Greezy was such a vile, disgusting town hardly anyone new had moved there in centuries. So for hundreds of years Greezians had married other Greezians until everyone was closely related, more or less.

Except for one woman who could not have been more different.

The other Greezians were short and squat, with rolls of jelly around their middles. But this woman was tall and thin, with a pinched face and a sharp nose. Her eyes were uncrossed and her black hair was dragged into a tight onion on the top of her head. And she was marching towards the car with purpose.

Even with the windows wound tight shut and the car doors locked, Danny could taste the menace that oozed from the woman's skin. An invisible cloud of doom hovered above her head. Her shadow sucked the joy from life.

Danny's heart stopped beating.

He knew who she was.

It was Aunty Ratbag.

Chapter 5

AUNTY RATBAG

SOME PARENTS THREATEN their naughty children with the bogeyman. Stop fighting, their mummies and daddies tell them, or the bogeyman will snatch you up and eat you. Other families have bears or wolves or little green men from Mars.

In Danny's family it was Aunty Ratbag.

Danny had never met his aunt – until that moment he did not believe that Aunty Ratbag could be a real person – but he recognised her at once from Mr Bouygues' description. The face was unmistakable: the bloodless lips, the jutting chin, the nose twisted as if she had smelt a fart in church and the cruel eyes that said she knew the fart was yours.

And suddenly Danny understood why he was in Greezy. This was his punishment for the Crown Jewels being found under his bed. And Danny's punishment was a thousand times worse than the life sentence the judge had given to Mr and Mrs Bouygues. He had been sent to live with Aunty Ratbag.

The lady in the green coat had also seen Aunty Ratbag.

'About blooming time!' she growled, striding the garden path. 'Keep me waiting will you, you stupid old hag.' And she began to rehearse the torrent of rude words she would hurl at Aunty Ratbag for not being at home to meet them.

The foolish, self-deluded woman. Blinded by fury, the lady in the green coat missed the multiplying signs of danger. The street had emptied. As Aunty Ratbag approached the Greezians fled, mothers abandoning their prams in the rush to escape. The bawling infant occupants fell instantly silent when the shadow of Aunty Ratbag passed them. Quiet spread down the street. Even the birds stopped tweeting. Time itself seemed to have slowed.

The lady in the green coat was oblivious. All she saw was just an old woman who did not own a fashionable raincoat.

'How dare you...!' she began. Then the shadow reached her and the lady in the green coat changed her mind. The rude words dried in her throat. Her jaw dropped, her chins wobbled. Her only thought was how to escape, and fast.

With twitching, fumbling fingers, she rooted through her handbag amongst the crusty hankies and lipsticks and chocolate bars, searching for her car keys.

'Why did you put them in your bag?' she squeaked. 'Why didn't you keep them in your hand?'

She found the car keys and dropped them. Her fumbling fingers had no strength to grip. She found them again and, holding the keys in both hands, she pressed the button on the fob that unlocked the car door.

Clunk!

The doors unlocked.

Clunk!

Her panicking fingers had pressed the button again, relocking the doors.

Not realising her mistake, the lady in the green coat yanked the door handle.

'Noooooo!' she wailed and she pressed the button again, and again and again and again.

Clunk!Clunk!Clunk!Clunk!Clunk!Clunk!Clunk!Clunk!

She pulled the handle again and again and again, but only when the door was locked.

And with every *Clunk!* Aunty Ratbag was drawing closer.

'Please!' she begged, pleading to Danny through the closed window of the locked car door.

Danny did not hesitate for a second. The lady in the green coat was horrible, but that did not matter now. She was a fellow creature in mortal danger and Mr Bouygues had taught Danny that, when lives are at stake, disagreements, even between the worst of enemies, should be forgotten. 'Do the right thing,' Mr Bouygues explained patiently. 'And hope they will too.'

The French are wiser. *'Elp yo ainormees perhaps,'* was Mrs Bouygues' advice. *'But never truzz'd zem.'*

On the next *Clunk!* Danny pulled the handle and pushed the car door wide open before the stupid bum-faced woman could re-lock it.

Danny should have listened to his mother because the lady in the green coat did not hesitate for even half a second. She reached into the car, grabbed Danny's arm, dragged him out of the car and threw him sprawling onto the pavement.

'He's yours,' she squeaked as she jumped into the front seat behind the steering wheel.

She jammed the car keys into the ignition and gunned the engine. In a cloud of stinking burning rubber that reminded Danny of his mother's croissants, the lady in the green coat roared away, driving wildly and crashing into parked cars and dustbins, smashing her car's headlights and ripping the bumpers clean off. The lady in the green coat did not care. Killing her car was a price worth paying just as long as she escaped!

It was many hours later, when she had put one hundred miles between herself and Aunty Ratbag, when the lady in the green coat discovered quite how terrified she had been. In her fright she had peed in her knickers. She had been so scared she had not noticed before.

To steady her nerves, the lady in the green coat stopped at the next motorway station and ate a chocolate bar, biting great chunks and chomping with her mouth open. Dribbles of brown saliva leaked from her lips dripped from her chins, leaving a stain on her coat she could never wash away.

As she slowly recovered her wits, the lady in the green coat began to think: if just seeing Aunty Ratbag was enough to make a grown woman wee herself, how long could a child survive living in the same house?

Her face turned as green as her coat. She knew the answer to her own question. There was no hope for Danny. Within a week he would either be mad or dead.

A better person would have felt a pang of guilt for delivering a defenceless child to such a wicked woman. A braver person would have returned to rescue him. But the lady in the green coat was neither good nor brave. She was mean and cowardly. So she wiped her chins, put the car into gear and clank-clank-clanked away, leaving Danny Bouygues to his fate.

Chapter 6

WELCOME TO HELL

BACK IN THE grim and grimy streets of Greezy, Aunty Ratbag had reached her destination. She emerged through the fog of burning rubber – the metal nails in the soles of her black boots crack-cracking on the pavement and striking sparks – and found Danny face down on the ground before her, defenceless.

She grinned and her eyes glittered unnaturally. The lenses in Aunty Ratbag's eyeballs were made of glass. Her real lenses – the living ones she had been born with – had turned milky white with rage. A surgeon had cut them out or she would have gone blind. Aunty Ratbag did not thank the surgeon for saving her eyesight. She kicked him in the shin and made the nurses cry.

Aunty Ratbag took a final step and stopped when the tips of her heavy boots were kissing the tips of Danny's out-stretched pink fingers. Around her ankles a pack of tiny dogs snapped and snarled and bared their needle teeth at the fallen boy. Aunty Ratbag had been walking the dogs in the park. Not for their exercise. Aunty Ratbag did not care about her pets' health and happiness. It was so the dogs could poo where children played.

And Aunty Ratbag _never_ scooped.

There were six of the unlovely creatures, with hairless mottled diseased-looking skin, naked except for the silly tufts of white fluff on the ends of their ears and tails. The dogs' characters matched their looks. They were vain, spiteful and pathetic.

Inside his head Danny whispered a desperate prayer: Please, please be nice and I promise I'll never be bad ever again!

Aunty Ratbag peered down her long, thin nose and examined the child lying prone at her feet. Danny shivered. As Aunty Ratbag's cyborg eyes moved over him, Danny felt his Aunt's inhuman vision slicing through his skin and peeling back his flesh and reaching deep into his body. He felt her eyes rummaging about amongst his guts and liver and kidneys, until she found his spinal cord and followed the nervous thread into Danny's brain.

And for the first time in his life Danny knew real fear. With absolute certainty Danny knew that there was nothing he could hide from Aunty Ratbag. His hopes and dreams. His every thought and memory – good and bad. Aunty Ratbag saw everything. Even his most secret secret that was so secret Danny hardly dared admit it to himself.

Aunty Ratbag raised a iron-shod boot and brought it gently down to rest on the fingertips of Danny's outstretched right hand. She was careful not to crush his fingers, not yet, because Aunty Ratbag understood the science of torture. If torture were a subject taught in schools, Aunty Ratbag would write the textbook. And chapter one would teach her students that, sometimes, the anticipation of pain is worse than the real thing.

'Are you listening, boy?' she hissed. His aunt's voice made Danny think of a cat playing with a mouse. And every mouse knows how the game ends: badly for the mouse.

Danny nodded, clenching his eyes tight shut.

'Understand this, boy. I hate your father, I hate your mother and I hate you. You're not welcome here. You deserve to live on the streets in a cardboard box and scavenge food from bins!'

Danny gulped. He felt sick and dizzy. He had never believed Aunty Ratbag was a real person, anymore than he believed in the bogeyman or alien invaders from Mars. But Mr Bouygues had been telling the truth! And if only a quarter of his stories were true, Aunty Ratbag would still be the worst aunty there has ever been and ever could be.

'But that would bring even more disgrace on my family, so I'll take you into my house. But trust me, Danny *Bogey*, if you do one thing wrong – just one thing once – if you cross me or answer back or cause me the teeniest, tiniest *pinch* of trouble, I'll put you in there!'

Aunty Ratbag jabbed a finger at something across the road. Lying on the pavement, with his right hand trapped under his aunt's left boot, and with his eyes clamped shut, Danny had no idea where she was pointing. It could have been Grimm's or Slugg's or the graveyard. He did not know which was worst.

Aunty Ratbag smiled. She had practiced her welcome speech for hours, carefully crafting every phrase and gesture. No Hollywood actress could have delivered it half so well because an actress would have been pretending, whereas Aunty Ratbag meant every word.

Aunty Ratbag lifted her boot from Danny's fingers and stepped over the trembling boy. She opened the scabby front door and went inside her dark house, followed by her ugly dogs that scampered over Danny, leaving a trail of muddy footprints across the boy's back.

Danny struggled to his feet and took a wobbly step towards the door.

'Not you!' snapped Aunty Ratbag. 'Children of criminals use the back entrance!'

Then she slammed the door in his face.

Danny stood on the doorstep of the ugliest house in England. The foul polluted air was making his eyes sting and leak drops of salty water.

Or were they tears? Whatever they were, Danny wiped them away with his sleeve.

What should he do? Danny wanted to run away, but where could he go? He was the child of the most hated thieves in England. The whole world was against him. No one wanted him. No one loved him.

What other choice did he have?

Inside his head, Danny heard Mr Bouygues speaking: *'Beggars can't be choosers.'* So Danny summoned his last dregs of courage and forced his legs to quit their trembling and carry him through the narrow passageway that led to the rear of Aunty Ratbag's house.

When he reached the kitchen door Danny paused and took a deep breath. He swallowed and steeled himself to do what had to be done.

Danny knocked. As his knuckles struck the wood they made a hollow, echoing sound as if he was banging on the lid of a coffin. And he had a horrible feeling that it might be his.

Chapter 7

THE RULES

B EING GOOD AT being bad is easy. Almost anyone can do it. But being truly evil requires practice. Lots of practice.

Aunty Ratbag was naturally very horrid. She was cruel as a spider. Few humans in history have been half as mean. But when it came to acts of unspeakable nastiness Aunty Ratbag had gotten rather rusty.

Twenty years ago Aunty Ratbag had been extremely good at being extremely bad. If there was an Olympic medal for evil, Aunty Ratbag would have won the gold, the silver and the bronze because back then she had lots of practice. Twenty-four hours every day, seven days a week and fifty-two weeks a year. And on whom did she practise? On Lionel Gruntfuttock, Danny's father.

When he was a young boy, younger than Danny was now, Lionel's parents – Danny's English grandparents – had died in a car crash. It was a double tragedy for Lionel Gruntfuttock. First, he lost the parents whom he loved dearly and who loved him back twice as much. And second, the grieving boy was sent to live with his aunt.

The tragedy for Lionel was a dream come true for Aunty Ratbag. It was every Christmas and birthday and Easter and Halloween rolled into one and dipped in chocolate and sprinkled with toasted almonds. At last she had a child of her own to torment and confuse! Until then she had made do with her neighbours' cross-eyed brats: knocking them off their bicycles and bending the wheels; stabbing their footballs with scissors; poisoning their pets with weed killer; and slapping their faces when they cried. Pitiful stuff that any ordinary horrid person could do.

With the arrival of Lionel Gruntfuttock, finally, her true character could blossom. And it did, growing into an abominable rose with a deathly perfume.

Danny's dad lived with Aunty Ratbag for five long years. They were the worst five years any boy has ever known. But for Aunty Ratbag they were the very best.

The vile woman devoted herself to the task of making every moment of his existence a waking nightmare. She bruised his young body with slaps and pinches, and attacked his self-confidence with cutting remarks and humiliations. She gave him jobs he could never complete and, when he failed to complete them, she called him a *'lazy-good-for-nothing-waste-of-space!'* and pinched his arm. Then she gave him another impossible job so she could pinch his other arm.

Aunty Ratbag was so proud of her cruelty that she kept a diary to record every nasty trick. Her favourite prank was pouring cold tea over Lionel's pyjama bottoms when the little boy was fast asleep, exhausted after a day of unrelenting toil and punishment. Come the morning she would accuse him of wetting his bed and tease him until he cried. It scarred Mr Bouygues for life. Even now, twenty years later, when he fell asleep in his prison cell, Mr Bouygues was not sure if he would wake up in dry pyjamas.

At night, lying propped up in her bed, Aunty Ratbag would

read her diary out loud. It never ceased to make her chortle and the tales of wickedness inspired her sleeping mind to devise fresh horrors.

Then, one dreadful night, Lionel ran away.

Aunty Ratbag could never forget the awful scene: the empty room; the open window; and the knotted rope made from a blanket torn into ragged strips. She thought she would never laugh again.

Then the miracle happened. The Bouygues were flung into prison and Danny was literally thrown at her feet! It was a second chance of happiness, made doubly sweet because, in addition to the pleasures of tormenting Danny, she would be taking her revenge on Mr Bouygues for running away and spoiling her fun.

Aunty Ratbag slammed the door in Danny's startled face and leapt in the air, cracking the heels of her boots together. 'Whoopee!' she screeched. 'Hurrah! Maybe there is a Tooth Fairy after all!'

Then she pulled herself together.

'There's no time for celebration, Mavis Gruntfuttock. You've got work to do!'

Aunty Ratbag bounded up the staircase, five steps at a time. She had old lady's legs, but evil had kept her wizened muscles quick and agile, and immensely strong. Her stick-thin arms had the power of a mountain gorilla. With her bare hands, Aunty Ratbag could rip spring lambs apart, to keep fit or just for fun. The local farmers knew it was Aunty Ratbag who murdered their flocks by night, but they were too scared to tell the police. It would have made no difference if they had because the police were just too scared to arrest her.

In her bedroom Aunty Ratbag took a small key from a secret place and unlocked the battered metal trunk at the foot of her bed. The metal trunk was where she kept her diary and other special mementoes. Like the mousetraps she had hid in the fridge and kitchen cupboards to stop Mr Bouygues stealing extra food. The sharp stick she poked him with when he fell asleep doing jobs. The mummified kitten she slipped under his pillow whenever he lost a tooth. A cheery teapot shaped like a cherry bun. And Mr Bouygues' old school uniform, a one-piece hodgepodge of different coloured and textured fabrics cut from her old dresses or stolen from scarecrows.

Aunty Ratbag held the uniform up to the light to admire her handiwork. It was a masterpiece of evil fashion. A circus clown would be embarrassed to wear it! The arms and legs were trimmed to slightly different lengths - Aunty Ratbag had experimented to achieve the most embarrassing combination. In place of a tie, a purple sock was glued to the collar and instead of sewing the bits of rag together with cotton thread, Aunty Ratbag had stapled them, which made the uniform look even more ridiculous.

The uniform was rough and itchy, and it had rubbed Mr Bouygues in delicate places and given him a nasty rash.

Unfortunately, it was too small for Danny.

'He's been overfed,' Aunty Ratbag cursed. 'His blasted father's spoiled him! But I'll fix that soon enough. And until the boy looses a few pounds, I can staple some extra scraps here and there,' she told herself. 'I'll have it ready for his second week at school.'

Aunty Ratbag chuckled at the thought of school. Mr Bouygues' teachers had punished him for not wearing the

proper uniform. In the playground the other children had teased him mercilessly.

'And schools are even nastier nowadays,' she smirked. 'So the teasing your father endured will be nothing compared to what you'll suffer, Danny Bouygues!'

Beneath the uniform, on the bare metal base of the trunk, was Aunty Ratbag's greatest treasure. It was a wooden picture frame, about the size of a children's picture book. But there were no bright drawings behind the glass. There was just a rectangle of once white cotton yellowed with age and neatly stitched with black lies. It was *The Rules*.

Aunty Ratbag composed *The Rules* when Danny's dad had first arrived to live with her. They used to hang on a hook above the kitchen table, until he ran away. Aunty Ratbag was so distraught she had hidden *The Rules* in her trunk. There was still a faint pale patch on the wallpaper.

Clutching the picture frame to her chest, Aunty Ratbag hurried to the kitchen and re-hung *The Rules* on the hook. Then she opened the back door and asked Danny to come inside.

'You! Boy! Get in here and sit down! Over there and sharpish or you'll feel the back of my hand, you lazy good for nothing filthy brat!'

Aunt Ratbag jabbed a finger towards a four-legged stool at the far end of the kitchen table near the bin. The stool was another clever invention of Aunty Ratbag's subtle mind. She had shaved its legs to different lengths, so no matter how still the sitter sat, the stool always wobbled and the sitter felt unbalanced, tipping first one way then the other.

Aunty Ratbag gave Danny a few moments to get properly uncomfortable. Then she sat down on the chair opposite Danny – a straight-backed even-legged chair - and glared at the boy, daring him to hold her gaze. Danny dropped his eyes to the floor and Aunty Ratbag snorted, pleased that the boy had already learned who wore the trousers in this house. And who would wear the clown uniform made from old dresses and scarecrow's rags.

Smirking nastily, Aunty Ratbag screwed one of her home-made cigarettes between her thin lips. Aunty Ratbag was too mean to buy her smokes from shops. Instead she made her own using the nettles and other weeds that grew in her garden, which she rolled in pages torn from library books – always the last page of exciting thrillers. They burned with a rancid stench.

Aunty Ratbag struck a match and held the flame to the tip of her weed cigarette. She puff-puff-puffed to get her ciggie burning strongly and, when the tip was glowing white hot, she took a long deep suck and filled her lungs with grey smog. Slowly she exhaled and a cloud of smoke rolled across her tongue and filtered through the gaps between her brown teeth. Scraps of meat were caught in some of the gaps. Years of smoking had cured the flesh into bacon.

'Look at me, boy.'

Danny could not stop himself obeying his aunt's command, although the sight of the horrible woman filled him with dread. The way the smoke drifted from Aunty Ratbag's mouth made him think of a midnight graveyard in a horror film. Her teeth were the tombstones and who knows what monsters lurked beneath her tongue.

Aunty Ratbag sucked hard and the cigarette flared and burning thistle seeds crackled and popped.

'Are you listening carefully?'

Danny blinked. It was all he could do. His eyelids were the only part of his body that he still controlled.

'Then I'll begin. I've taken you into my house out of the goodness of my heart...'

There was no goodness in Aunty Ratbag's heart.

'...and because you're *family*...'

In Aunty Ratbag's mouth *'family'* sounded like the worst swear word.

'...I'll feed and clothe you out of my own pocket. But you'll earn your keep, my lad. This is a large house and there are plenty of jobs to do and you'll do every last one. And I won't put up with any complaints or moaning. And if you don't like it, you can clear off and find someone else to look after you. Although you won't find anyone half nice as me, you disgusting little worm!'

One of Aunty Ratbag's greatest gifts when it came to being unspeakably cruel was her ability to scramble truth with lies until it was impossible to separate one from the other.

The Bouygues' rose-covered cottage and the restaurant had been sold, and the money had gone into a bank account to pay for Danny's needs. There was more than enough to feed and clothe him properly, but Aunty Ratbag had no intention of wasting the money on Danny. She was planning to steal every penny for herself.

And there were plenty of good people who would have looked after Danny with kindness and would not blame him for his parents' crimes. The police were going to send Danny to one of those sorts of people - reluctantly - until Aunty Ratbag had 'phoned and insisted that she should have the boy because, as she had told the police, he was family.

'Whilst you're living under my roof,' continued Aunty Ratbag, blowing jets of smoke through her nostrils. 'You will obey my rules. Can you read or are you another idiot like your father?'

'I can read,' Danny mumbled. Mr Bouygues had taught him to read and write in English before he had started school. And Mrs Bouygues had taught him reading and writing in her native French. And the Spanish and Italian she spoke as fluently as a resident of Madrid or Rome. And the dozen other languages she spoke nearly as well. But not German because, according to Mrs Bouygues, *'Germonne ez an urg'lee long weege.'*

'Then read these.'

Aunty Ratbag pointed at *The Rules*.

'Out loud so I know you're not lying. Your father was a liar, so I expect you are too.'

Aunty Ratbag rose to her feet and stalked around the kitchen table to stand close behind Danny on wobbling stool. Leaning close to his ear, she blew thick smog though his hair. She meant to make him cough, but Danny hardly noticed. Aunty Ratbag's homemade fags were sweeter than his mother's French cigarettes.

Danny began to read.

> 'Rule 1. My beloved Aunt is ALWAYS right, especially when she is wrong.
>
> Rule 2. I am always wrong - ALWAYS – even when I am right.
>
> Rule 3. I must never speak unless spoken to.
>
> Rule 4. One square of toilet paper is sufficient.
>
> Rule 5. Two squares are a wasteful extravagance.
>
> Rule 6. Using three squares is a crime punishable by INSTANT DEATH.
>
> Rule 7. Laughing is strictly forbidden. So are smiling or thinking happy thoughts.
>
> Rule 8. I don't deserve food until ALL my jobs are finished.
>
> Rule 9. If I am not waiting on the doorstep at 6 o'clock sharp with my hands scrubbed clean, it is my own fault if I am locked outside and made to stay in the shed to sleep with the rats and spiders.
>
> Rule 10. I am strictly forbidden ON PAIN OF INSTANT DEATH from entering my Aunt's house

*without her permission and until 6 o'clock I will
NEVER be given permission, even if it's raining or
snowing or hailing or blowing a hurricane.*

*Rule 11. Every room is out of bounds, except the
kitchen and my bedroom.*

Rule 12. When I am punished it is for my own good.

*Rule 13. I must be grateful at all times for my beautiful
Aunt's extraordinary kindness and generosity for
giving me a loving family home.*

*Rule 14. Lastly, I must always remember that I am a
disgusting brat who deserves everything I get.'*

Danny finished reading, but he did not understand. Not the
words and the sentences. He understood those well enough.
He could translate them into fifteen languages if Aunty Ratbag
asked him to. It was their meaning. How could anyone –
especially a grown up – be so unfair? Danny's parents had never
been unfair. If anything, Mr Bouygues had been too fair. Mr
Bouygues *always* gave Danny the benefit of the doubt, even
when he *must* have known that Danny was telling a whopping
fib.

Also some of *The Rules* did not make sense, like the one
about the whole house being out of bounds except his
bedroom and the kitchen.

'What if I need the toilet?'

'Use the garden,' growled Aunty Ratbag. 'If it's good
enough for my dogs, it's good enough for you.' Then she
wacked him on the back of his head. 'For breaking Rule 3,'
she explained.

Danny was stunned. Not by the blow itself. It was the shock

of being hit. His parents had *never* slapped him. Not once. Not even when he borrowed Mr Bouygues' car and drove it into the duck pond. Although on that occasion Mr Bouygues' came as close to being cross as he could manage. Petrol leaked from the tank and poisoned the water bugs and made his road kill pancakes taste disgusting. Mrs Bouygues had shooed her husband away and took Danny up to his bedroom to change and told him not to worry.

'Eez yo' fazzer's foalt,' she had said. *'Ee shoon'tav tote yo' ow toe dryve onteal yo' woz towel enuv toe zee o'vair ze steerwingreel. On ee way, eez only a Germonne kar.'*

For reasons Danny had never properly understood, Mrs Bouygues did not like Germans or their cars.

Behind Danny's head, Aunty Ratbag raised her hand ready to strike again.

'Are we hungry?' she asked

Danny almost fell into her trap. He was starving. He had not eaten since he had left Scotland Yard and that was hours ago. The mere mention of food was enough to start his stomach rumbling.

Danny opened his mouth to say 'yes' when he remembered *Rule 3*.

Had he been spoken to? Or was Aunty Ratbag speaking to herself? Or to her dogs? Or was it one of those rhetorical sort of questions that are not really questions? Danny was not sure, so he decided to play safe; to keep his mouth shut and nod his head.

Aunty Ratbag's eyes narrowed. Had Danny seen through her trick? Or was he just struck dumb with fear? Never mind, she thought. She would find another reason to slap him soon enough.

'Goody,' she hissed. 'Because I've planned something special for your first supper in your new home. It was your father's favourite meal. I hope you like it.'

Aunty Ratbag had bought a meat pie for her own supper. It was already cooking in the oven. The label on the pie box said it was made with *tender chunks of prime beef cooked in a rich red wine gravy*. Which was nearly all lies because the pie was made in a secret kitchen hidden in the basement beneath Grimm's Dog Food Factory. The *prime beef* was mainly horse and seaside donkey, and the *tender chunks* were the scraps of gristle that were so disgusting even dogs would not eat them. The only *beef* were the hooves of ancient milkers boiled into the gluey gravy.

There were enough donkeys' eyelids and cows' hoof to feed three or even four hungry adults. But Aunty Ratbag preferred not to share. She had something much nastier planned for Danny's supper.

From the freezer she took three stalks of frozen broccoli, dropped them into a tin bowl and filled the bowl to the brim with cold tap water. Then she placed the bowl in front of Danny.

Danny stared at the bowl and the three stalks of broccoli floating on the surface like miniature trees.

'What is it?' he asked.

'Soup!' snapped Aunty Ratbag as she slapped him for breaking Rule 3.

When Danny had finished his cold broccoli soup he followed Aunty Ratbag upstairs to his bedroom. It was a dismal space. There was no bed to sleep on, just a hard wooden floor, and a blanket made from long strips of material that had been stapled together. The window was barred inside and out and nailed shut. There were no curtains, so the light of the nearly full moon flooded in. The moon was the only light because Aunty Ratbag had removed the electric light fitting. A bare wire dangled from the ceiling, emitting an occasional blue spark.

'Sleep well,' smirked Aunty Ratbag as she closed the door. 'I hope you'll be comfortable.'

Then she locked the door with two keys, a padlock and three heavy bolts, and, to be extra safe, wedged a chair under the handle.

Danny listened to Aunty Ratbag's footsteps clumping down the stairs and to the sound of laughter when she switched on the TV. Danny recognised the programme. He used to watch it with his parents on Saturday evenings, the three of them curled up on the sofa, in front of an open fire, eating earwigs fried in honey.

Imprisoned and hungry, Danny should have felt more lonely and miserable than any child in the world. He should have done, but he did not. But only because he was already fast asleep.

So Danny did not hear the new sound coming from downstairs.

Click! Click! Click!

Aunty Ratbag had found her stapler.

Chapter 8

THE SCIENCE OF EVIL AND BOILING FROGS

IT WAS AFTER midnight and Aunty Ratbag was sitting in bed smoking a thistle cigarette. Beside her the six hairless dogs snoozed uneasily, especially the mutt lying closest to Aunty Ratbag because the prized spot came with a high risk. If something should anger her, Aunty Ratbag's gentle strokes would become a choking squeeze and her long fingernails would cut through naked skin. And if she was really furious, she might snatch the creature up and hurl the unfortunate dog at the bedroom wall. It had happened before, many times. There was space for fifteen dogs on her bed. A pattern of stains on the wallpaper was all that remained of the others.

For now, though, the dogs were safe because their mistress was engrossed in her favourite book and the happy memories it contained. She had almost forgotten how creatively cruel she could be.

Aunty Ratbag blew a perfect smoke ring and turned to the next page in her diary. She read a few lines and grinned. It was the entry she had written on the night of Mr Bouygues' 7th birthday. Aunty Ratbag had organised a surprise party and invited all the boys and girls from Lionel Bouygues' class. The 'surprise' was the food and entertainment. The guests were fed dog food sandwiches and cat food brownies, whilst Lionel ate pizza and chocolate cake, and the games were rigged so

he won every prize. Of course the children took their revenge at the first opportunity. Aunty Ratbag sniggered at the memory of boy's bruised face when he returned home from school the following day.

Aunty Ratbag turned to the next page and found an even nastier trick. And after that a worse one, and then a worser one yet, because Aunty Ratbag's cruelty was not random. Every nasty act was part of a diabolical experiment. An experiment she called *The Boiled Frog*.

When she was a little girl, with pigtails and freckles, Aunty Ratbag had amused herself by killing small animals. She started with ants, toasting them with a magnifying glass until they popped. Later, when she grew bored with ants, she switched to butterflies and beetles, pulling off their wings and legs, or impaling them on pins.

Lots of small children enjoy killing bugs. It is a habit most of them out grow, but not Aunty Ratbag. She had progressed to larger things, like mice and songbirds and her neighbours' pets. When, by accident, she made an interesting scientific discovery.

When she threw live frogs into boiling water, the frogs leapt straight out. Aunty Ratbag had to put the lid on the saucepan to stop them escaping. However, if she put the croakers into cold water then slowly raised the temperature, the frogs were unaware of their peril until it was too late. The frogs swam in circles, even as the water began to steam and bubble, until they were completely cooked.

Aunty Ratbag applied the same scientific technique to breaking Danny's father. When Lionel Gruntfuttock first arrived she pretended to be kind. She gave him a warm bed and hearty meals and hugs and kisses. 'Nice' in Aunty Ratbag's opinion. The bed was hard and lumpy, the meals were tasteless gloop and her hugs made him squirm. The feel of her squidgy bits beneath her dress squelching against him were worse than any deliberate torture.

Then, slowly, Aunty Ratbag turned up the heat.

The bowls of gloop grew smaller and, one by one, his possessions began to disappear. First to go were his toys and books, then the duvet and the pillows and sheets, the curtains, the light bulb and, finally, the bed.

When Aunty Ratbag replaced his clothes with the stapled uniform, he accepted the change without complaint. The first time he failed to complete his chores, the boy bore the mild punishment in silence and, the following day, worked harder. But the list of jobs had increased by one. And so the cycle went on and on, with the chance of finishing his chores becoming fractionally more impossible and the punishments getting steadily meaner, until Aunty Ratbag was sure she had won.

Except Danny's dad had jumped from the pot before he was quite cooked.

Like any proper scientist, although Aunty Ratbag was disappointment that her experiment had failed, she accepted the results. Human beings were not as stupid as frogs, except Greezians who had less brainpower than newts. To break Danny, she would have to try a different technique.

Unfortunately, for Danny, Aunty Ratbag had already devised a new experiment. This time, instead of gradually turning up the heat, she would fling Danny into a metaphorical pot of boiling water, then pluck him out and smother him with kindness. And when the boy felt safe, she would throw him back into the pot! One day she would be horrid and the next lovely. Horrid, lovely, horrid, lovely, horrid, lovely. Then horrid, horrid, horrid, followed by lovely, lovely, lovely until Danny was so confused he would not know which way was up.

'What shall I be tomorrow?' she asked her dogs. 'Nice or nasty?'

Chapter 9

SUNDAY, THE DAY OF REST

DANNY BOUYGUES WOKE at dawn when the sun crept above the slated roof of Slugg's Cat Food Factory and peeked between the smoke-belching chimneys.

Danny always woke up early because dawn was his favourite time of day. It is a secret known only to a lucky few that the world is at its most beautiful before it is seen by too many people.

At least that is what Mr Bouygues told him when he ripped the duvet off his sleeping son and tumbled Danny out of bed. In the rose-covered cottage it was Danny's job to milk the goats and feed the rabbits-that-weren't-pets and search the field next door for cowpats and collect fresh the dung beetles for breakfast. To finish his chores before he left for school, Danny had no choice except to get up with the sun. And being a sensible sort of child, Danny had learned to love what he could not avoid.

Danny yawned and stretched until his joints popped. And to his enormous surprise, he discovered that, despite everything that had happened, he was happy to be alive.

Today is a new day, Danny told himself. And no matter what happens, it can't be worse than yesterday.

Danny examined his new accommodation. It was not a patch on his bedroom in the Bouygues' cottage. That had been filled with fantastical furniture built by Mrs Bouygues using bits of driftwood she found on beaches. Mrs Bouygues fitted the sea-polished pieces together like a 3D jigsaw, so cleverly that she did not need nails or glue. Danny's bed was crusty with salt, and encrusted with scraps of dried seaweed and barnacles. In his dreams his bed carried him on voyages to desert islands. It was unfair to compare any other room to that. But at least this one had improved overnight. The sun shinning through the orange window was painting the walls a rosy gold and taking the edge of the chill.

And it was *his* room, which mattered. His cell in Scotland Yard was a windowless box and the bright lights were switched on night and day. A video camera had watched his every move. A room without a bed or electric lights is better than that. And, anyway, who needs lights when you've got your own window!

Danny jumped to his feet and peered through the panes of smeary orange glass. He was oddly excited. He had never woken up in a city. What would he find? In the rose-covered cottage it was the same view every morning: fields and woods, a stream, cows, wild deer and pheasants.

His eyes adjusted to the sunlight and…

'Oh dear.'

Danny's bubble of optimism popped on the sharp pin of reality. His underground cell in Scotland Yard was better than this.

Danny had forgotten that Aunty Ratbag's house over-looked the graveyard. Usually Danny was not disturbed by graveyards and the thought of the dead bodies lying under the soil. There was a church next to the Bouygues' restaurant and Danny had often played with friends in the churchyard.

The stone memorials made excellent hiding places and the old people who placed flowers on their loved ones' graves were happy to see children laughing, provided the children were respectful. But the churchyard was a warm, sunny place, filled with lazy bees and perfumed with honeysuckle and shaded by ancient yews. Greezy's graveyard was different. There were no bees or flowers or a single tree. The tombstones were darkened with thick layers of congealed factory smog. None stood straight and they were crammed together, so close that the stones were almost touching.

Danny gulped. If there was one stone for each body then the bodies of the dead must be piled on top of each other, packed as close as sausages, with eight or nine or ten skeletons sharing every grave.

As he looked at the grim scene, Danny felt an electric tingle on the back of his neck. Someone was watching him. Danny did not know how he knew, but he was certain.

His eyes searched amongst the tombstones. Suddenly, he found the watcher. It was an old man, dressed in a shabby nut-brown tweed jacket with patches on the elbows and green moleskin trousers tucked into black wellingtons. His trousers and boots were splattered with mud, some of it fresh, but most of it dry and flaking. The man was leaning on a spade beside an open hole seven feet long and two feet wide. He was staring straight at Danny.

It was the gravedigger.

CRASH! The bedroom door smashed open.

'WHAT ARE YOU DOING?'

It was Aunty Ratbag. She had silently drawn the bolts and burst in hoping to frighten him.

Danny span around.

'N-n-nothing, Aunty,' he stammered, feeling guilty although he could not think why he should.

'You horrible brat!' screamed Aunty Ratbag. She had been looking forward to ripping the blankets off him. 'Get downstairs!' and she raised a threatening hand as Danny scampered past.

Aunty Ratbag was about to follow him when she stopped.

'What was the filthy brat looking at?' she muttered and she stepped close to the window to see for herself. Her sour breath misted the pane of orange glass.

The gravedigger had not moved. He was leaning on his spade by the open grave staring at the house, still and solid as the slabs of stone that surrounded him.

Their eyes locked in combat, challenging the other to give way. Aunty Ratbag glared at the gravedigger with all the menace she could muster, which was more than any other living person on planet earth. Her anger warmed the room like a radiator. And the gravedigger fought her back, stare for stare.

Aunty Ratbag blinked first. She always did.

'Damn and blast!' she cursed. In the whole of England the gravedigger was the only living soul who was not afraid of her. Which made her mood even fouler.

'Boy!' she shrieked as she stomped from the bedroom and slammed the door. 'I hope you're not enjoying yourself!'

*****

Danny waited in the kitchen, listening to his aunt's roars and the clomp-clomp of her heavy boots banging on the wooden stairs. He was trembling. Not just because he was scared. It was with the effort of trying and failing to balance on the wobbly stool.

Aunty Ratbag burst into the kitchen.

'Take these!' she snapped, tossing a green plastic bottle of pine-scented toilet cleaner and a thin rag at Danny's head.

'Errr?' spluttered Danny.

'For washing with, you idiot,' snarled Aunty Ratbag and she rolled her eyes as if using toilet cleaner like shower gel was so obvious that only a imbecile would have to ask. 'Your French mother might be dirty...'

Aunty Ratbag was the sort of English person who thinks that all foreigners are dirty, especially the French who are filthy beyond compare. Aunty Ratbag had never been to France – she had never left Greezy. But she knew she was right about foreigners in general and the French in particular for the same reason that Aunty Ratbag knew she was right about everything else. Because Aunty Ratbag could not believe that Aunty Ratbag could be wrong about anything. And if she was wrong, she did not care.

'... but in this house we wash before breakfast. Get outside! There's a tap in the garden by the shed. And make sure you turn it off when you've finished or I'll skin you alive and nail your miserable hide to the fence!'

The mean trickle of rust brown water that issued from the garden tap was icy and smelled faintly of rotten meat and fish. It had an unpleasant oily feel too. So did all the tap water in Greezy. Pollution had soaked into the earth and penetrated the water pipes.

Danny squirted toilet cleaner into his hands and rubbed

them together to make green froth. He had already stripped to his underpants and, using his hands for a flannel, he scrubbed himself all over: between his toes, behind his ears and under his arms. Danny liked being clean. It was a habit he had learned from his mother.

When he finished washing Danny's pine-scented skin was lumpy with goose bumps and his lips were turning purplish-blue. But he hardly noticed. Danny was used to washing outdoors in colder water than this. He had bathed in mountain streams fed by melting snow. Mr Bouygues said it would toughen him up.

Toughening Danny up was important to Mr Bouygues. So every weekend throughout the winter, unless it was unseasonably warm, Mr Bouygues took his son camping. Mrs Bouygues called them *'cray'zee rosbifs'* and stayed at home, curled up under her duvet, reading *Vogue* and eating Belgian chocolates, whilst Mr Bouygues and Danny cycled to the most inhospitable corners of the British Isles. Like the north shore of Scotland where the winter gales come howling off the Atlantic Ocean straight from the Arctic.

And he always chose the most exposed spot to pitch their tent. One winter, they had camped on the peaks of Brecon Beacons during a blizzard so severe that flocks of mountain sheep froze solid and British soldiers training on the hills had to be rescued by helicopter. When their ran out of food, Mr Bouygues boiled their leather walking boots to make soup. Boot soup was all they ate for a week. Luckily the soup was made by Mr Bouygues, so it was surprisingly good. If you can survive that, tap water that smells only faintly of rotting flesh is as good as a hot bath, and pine-scented toilet cleaner is an extravagant luxury.

Drying his face with a rag, Danny thought of their last camping trip. They had gone to Wales in January, Snowdonia this time. As usual, Mr Bouygues chose the most dangerous place to pitch their tent – an exposed mountaintop a dozen miles from the nearest village. An unexpected hurricane blasted in from the Irish Sea and tore away their tent and everything in it. Danny was still wearing his outdoor winter clothes and boots – but Mr Bouygues was getting changed for bed. All his clothes and underwear were blown across Wales and into Shropshire. Mr Bouygues and Danny had to tramp down the mountainside, bent double as they battled against the raging wind, to reach a remote cottage. Despite his winter clothes, Danny was stiff with cold, but Mr Bouygues was far worse. His whole body was blue with hypothermia and his hands were shivering so hard he had to press the doorbell with his nose.

The cottage belonged to a little Welsh granny who lived by herself with only a cat for company. She was so shocked, she almost forgot to invite them in. It was not her fault. Mr Bouygues had covered his private bits with a handful of wild grass that he had picked on the mountainside. Unfortunately, the wild grass was mainly thistles and nettles, and when the Welsh granny opened her door she found a naked blue Englishman dancing round her garden hooting in agony. Who would not stare and be forgetful of their manners?

They stayed with the old lady for five days, waiting for the hurricane to pass. Mr Bouygues asked if he could borrow some clothes, but the granny only spoke Welsh and she did not understand. She thought he wanted a small lacy apron and that was all she gave him to wear. When Mrs Bouygues arrived to collect them, the old lady blushed scarlet because, of course, she did speak English. She was only pretending not to. Mrs Bouygues told the granny not to worry. She said she was French so she understood and, when she was an old lady, if she ever got the chance she would do *'egg zackerlee ze zame'*.

After a cup of tea and some homemade Welsh cakes, Mrs Bouygues discovered that she had forgotten to bring any spare clothes for her husband. So Mr Bouygues had to travel home still dressed in the tiny apron. It did not matter very much when they were in the car. But when they stopped at a motorway service station outside Wolverhampton to use the toilet, Mr Bouygues blushed twice as scarlet as the little old lady.

Danny's face broke into a wide smile at the memory of the crowds of cheering lorry drivers pointing at Mr Bouygues and blasting their horns. And Mrs Bouygues laughing until she got the hiccups.

Aunty Ratbag was watching through the kitchen window. Normally she hated other people's happiness. Not this time. This time it thrilled her because only the strongest child could endure what Danny had suffered and still have the spirit to smile. And breaking that spirit was a challenge worthy of her talents.

Danny had single slice of dry bread for his breakfast, thrice-toasted and burned black to the core, without any jam or butter. And whilst Danny crunched his charcoal, Aunty Ratbag guzzled a traditional Greezy breakfast with all the trimmings: raw pigs' hearts and scrambled lambs' brains smothered in clotted cream, with a generous helping of prunes to help her bowels move.

When she had seconds and thirds of creamy, fruity offal, Danny wondered why she was not grossly fat. The reason was simple enough: Aunty Ratbag had caught worms from kissing her dogs and the wriggling parasites that lived in her belly re-ate most of the food that passed Aunty Ratbag's lips and kept her trim.

Aunty Ratbag swallowed the last lump of pinky-grey of lambs' brains and pushed her plate away and belched. Inside her guts the worms started on their feast.

Danny wobbled on his stool and waited.

'If you've finished gorging,' sneered Aunty Ratbag, picking at a chunk of prune that was stuck between her teeth. 'It's time to earn your keep.'

Aunty Ratbag had prepared a long list of jobs, carefully chosen to break Danny's spirit bit by bit.

The first task was not difficult. It was cleaning Aunty Ratbag's boots. Danny polished them until they shone like black diamonds. 'Useless!" complained Aunty Ratbag and she made him polish them again, twice.

Next he had to sweep and mop the floors throughout the house from top to bottom. Aunty Ratbag followed with her stick and poked him. Then it was brushing the dogs' teeth and combing their ears and tails. The dogs hated being groomed and although they were small and puny, their teeth were needle sharp. Their claws were tiny razors.

Aunty Ratbag lit a cigarette and chortled as Danny faced the pack of angry dogs armed with a toothbrush.

The dogs circled Danny, growling and barring their teeth and readying to pounce.

'Bit him, my beauties!' urged Aunty Ratbag.

Except Aunty Ratbag had forgotten that Danny was a country boy raised by a French woman who kept rabbits-that-weren't-pets. When the first dog leapt, Danny grabbed it by the neck – firmly, but without hurting the creature – clamped it under his arm so it could not scratch or bite, and pinched the hinge of the dog's jaws to open its mouth. The dog gave in without a whimper. The others fared no better.

Aunty Ratbag growled with disappointment and poked Danny for being rough with her pets.

Then it was time to do the ironing. Aunty Ratbag pointed to a large mound of dresses, sheets and pillowcases.

'Burn anything and I'll burn you!' snarled Aunty Ratbag.

Danny could tell that she meant it and, inside his head, he said a silent thank you to Mr Bouygues for teaching him how to use an electric iron. After years of practise, Danny's skills surpassed his father's. Even Aunty Ratbag was impressed with Danny's speed and precision. She whacked him anyway and threw the neat piles of ironing on the floor, stamped on them and made him start again.

The day was not going according to plan. The boy was insufferable! It was like someone had trained him to frustrate her evil plans. Never mind, she consoled herself. I'll break him this afternoon.

After a lunch of cold broccoli soup without the broccoli, Aunty Ratbag told Danny to keep his spoon. 'You'll need it for the next job,' she said as she shooed him into the back garden.

It was, without any doubt, the worst garden Danny had ever seen. It was more like a battlefield, a gruesome place of bare lifeless earth and scattered patches of rank weeds. A daily drizzle of dog piddle had poisoned the grass and the flowers, and drowned the worms. Only the toughest weeds had survived and between these prickly thickets, half buried in the mud, were the broken things Aunty Ratbag had thrown away: a fridge without a door, a busted washing machine, a TV with the screen punched in and the skeletons of nine tiny dogs.

And scattered everywhere were thousands upon thousands of dog eggs.

Some of the dog eggs had dried into hard white pebbles. Others were freshly laid and still moist and steaming. Some were alive with maggots or sprouting toadstools. Some were a feast for fat black slugs.

Aunty Ratbag gave Danny a plastic supermarket shopping bag.

'You'll need this,' she said. 'And mind you pick them all up. If you miss a single one, I'll rub your nose in it!'

Faced with such a task, most children would have held up their hands and sobbed. But most children do not grow up next to a dairy farm searching cowpats for dung beetles. And compared to those gigantic runny cow plops, the slug-infested dog eggs were puny things.

Danny quickly filled the shopping bag and asked for another and then another.

'Do you think I'm made of money?' complained Aunty Ratbag. 'They cost 5p each! That one's coming out of your pocket money!' she told him. Not that Aunty Ratbag was planning to give Danny any pocket money.

Armed with an empty shopping bag and his trusty soup spoon, Danny re-examined the garden. He had found all the obvious eggs. Now the real fun could begin; the search for the hidden ones!

In the rose-covered cottage it was Danny's job to collect the fresh chickens' eggs because even a kitchen wizard cannot change the taste and stink of a rotten egg. But finding the eggs was not easy. The Bouygues' hens free ranged from dawn to dusk and, although chickens are bird-brained, where their eggs are concerned they have a fool's cunning and they were always discovering new sneaky places to lay their clutches.

To win the game of eggy hide & seek Danny had learned to think like a chicken. Now he would have to think like a dog.

Danny squatted to get a dog's eye view of the garden. To hide their precious poops, some of the dogs had backed into the thickets of prickly weeds. Others had crawled behind the shed to do their dirty business. Some had squatted in the drums of the broken washing machine and inside the busted

TV, risking injury on the splinters of broken glass and rusted metal and twisted wires.

From his low angle, Danny could see all their secret hiding places.

'Got you!' he whispered and he leapt into action.

Spying through the kitchen window, Aunty Ratbag boiled with rage and frustration. 'Damn and blast!' she cursed. Her brain could not believe what her eyes were seeing. 'The dratted boy is enjoying himself!'

There was only had one job left. If could Danny finish this task, he had won.

'You'll need these,' snarled Aunty Ratbag and she gave Danny a bucket of soapy water, a sponge and a squeegee. 'Start at the front windows. And mind you clean them properly – no streaks - or you'll feel my stick on your lazy behind!'

Danny found a ladder in the shed. Half the rungs were cracked. The others were soft with rot. Danny heaved the ladder onto his shoulder and staggered through the passage-way to the front of the house. He leaned it against the wall, climbed carefully to the top, wet the sponge in soapy water and began to scrub.

Washing windows was a new experience for Danny. In the rose-covered cottage the men did all the household chores, except this one. 'Leave it to the rain,' Mr Bouygues would say. 'Windows clean themselves.'

As he sponged and squeegeed, Danny wondered why his father made such a fuss. The muck washed away easily and he enjoyed seeing the clean glass emerge and sparkle.

Danny finished the front windows and moved the ladder

to the back of the house. By now he was cold and wet. Soapy water had sploshed onto his clothes and dribbled down his arms, and the enjoyment of a job well done had long since passed.

Aunty Ratbag appeared just as Danny squeegeed the last pane of glass. Every window gleamed in the setting sun.

'Finished?' she asked, poking him in the bottom.

Danny nodded. He was too cold and weary to speak.

'No smudges or smears?'

Danny shook his head.

Aunty Ratbag chuckled. 'I think I'll be the judge of that.'

Danny followed Aunty Ratbag through the passageway...

...and gasped. The front windows that he had left sparkling clean were as dirty as before he started. Filth from the factory chimneys had re-oranged them whilst Danny was cleaning the windows at the back.

'You lying worm!' cackled Aunty Ratbag. 'Back up the ladder, you lazy brat! And don't come down until you've done a proper job!'

Danny re-climbed the ladder knowing that whilst he was re-polishing these windows factory filth was re-dirtying the others. Now Danny understood why Mr Bouygues hated cleaning windows because this was a job that would never end until Slugg's and Grimm's switched off their ovens and the chimneys ceased to smoke.

Chapter 10

GREEZY ACADEMY FOR FOOLS

THE FIRST DAY at a new school is always scary. When you arrive in the middle of term when everyone has made their friends and chosen where to sit it is even scarier. When you are the child of the most hated thieves in England and you have a surname that no one can forget, it is utterly terrifying.

Aunty Ratbag led the way, holding Danny by his ear so he could not escape. The shortest route to the school was along the path that cut through the middle of the graveyard. But Aunty Ratbag went the long way, around the edge of the graveyard, past Grimm's and the queue of lorries waiting, patiently, to deliver the ingredients that would be minced and boiled and turned into dog food. Inside the lorries, the ingredients - racehorses that had lost once too often and retired seaside donkeys – shuffled nervously.

She abandoned Danny at the school gate.

'And don't be late,' she warned him. 'If you're not back by 6 o'clock you can sleep in the shed.'

Danny gulped and crossed the wide playground alone.

The headmistress was expecting him. She was one of the cross-eyed Greezians and Danny did not know if she was looking at him or the floor or out the window or all three or somewhere else.

'I knew your father,' sneered the headmistress. 'Lionel Gruntfuttock was in my first class when I started teaching. You have the same weak chin and puny arms.'

Did his father have a weak chin and puny arms? Danny was not sure any more. It was so long since he had seen his parents that he was already forgetting. Then he remembered the car park of the motorway service station near Wolverhampton and Mr Bouygues dressed in a small apron and nothing else. Mr Bouygues was slim compared to the lorry drivers, but no one could call him puny. He was like a wolf with the fur shaved off: surprisingly skinny, but scarily strong.

'I always knew Lionel would turn out bad,' continued the headmistress, sounding delighted that her prediction had come true. 'He never fitted in. I expect you'll be the same. The apple doesn't fall far from the tree. Come with me, boy. I'll take you to your class.'

Danny followed the headmistress down gloomy corridors that had not seen a mop or a broom or a paintbrush in fifty years. Most of the light bulbs were broken and the few that worked flickered revealing grimy walls covered in graffiti pictures of a cross-eyed saggy-bottomed headmistress. Empty crisp and cigarette packets crunched underfoot, and the air smelled faintly of wee.

They passed the school trophy cupboard. The doors were hanging open, the glass was smashed and the silver cups long gone. The headmistress had stolen the cups and sold them to pay for the television in her office.

Further on, water leaking from the blocked girls' toilets had spread across the corridor forming an oily puddle. A pigeon floated feet up on the surface. The headmistress splashed through the middle, soaking her shoes and stockings. If she noticed, she did not seem to care.

Danny's classroom was on the other side of the puddle. The headmistress bashed the door open and squelched inside. For a moment Danny was blinded because the classroom was brighter than the corridor, with large orange-stained windows. It was smellier too; wee with a hint of dog egg.

The headmistress introduced him.

'This!' she bellowed pointing at Danny. 'This *beast*, this *worm* is Danny Boo-gees!'

In case the other children did not recognise his surname, the headmistress explained. 'It was his parents that stole the Crown Jewels. They've been sent to prison for the rest of their lives. It's less than they deserve. If it was up to me they would be hung in gibbets and left to fatten the crows!'

Half the children glared at Danny and other half glared out the window, or at the ceiling and the floor.

'I'm sure you will make him as unwelcome as he deserves. Carry on.'

The headmistress departed quickly, splashing through the puddle. She was in a hurry to get back to her office. Her favourite TV programme was about to start.

Danny gulped and shuffled his feet. As the squelching footsteps of the headmistress disappeared, Danny looked around the room and saw that the teacher and his new classmates were made from the same mould. They had the same fat round faces and pale waxy skin. Their copper-coloured hair was thick with grease and their middles circled with jelly. And at least half of them were cross-eyed.

Especially the big girl on the front row, who had the whitest waxiest skin, the greasiest orange hair, the fattest belly and the crossest-eyes in Greezy. She had spots too; hundreds of them. An archipelago of purple-sloped puss-filled zits were scattered across the waxy oceans of her cheeks and chin and her forehead. She had squeezed some of her pimples with dirty fingers spreading infection and these spots had swelled to volcanic proportions. A monster the size of a grape throbbed on the end of her nose.

She was the nastiest girl Danny had ever seen. He hated her at once and she hated him back.

'*Boo-Gees?*' said the teacher. '*Boo-Gees!* Is that a foreign name? I don't like foreigners.'

'It sounds like '*bogey*',' said the big girl. 'Danny Bogey! Let's call him that.'

The other children laughed rudely and so did the teacher.

'It's '*Bweeg*',' said Danny, interrupting. 'Not '*Boo-Gees*' or '*Bogey*'.' Danny was used to explaining his unusual surname. 'It's a French name. My mum's French.'

As soon as he said '*French*' Danny knew he had made a terrible mistake.

'FRENCH!' roared the teacher. 'FRENCH! Disgusting! The lad's a bloomin' frog!'

The children giggled because '*frog*' is a rude name for French people because some Frenchies like eating frogs' legs.

'Errrgh!' said the big girl. 'I hate frogs. They're slimy, like bogies. That's an even better name for the new boy. Let's call him Danny Slimy Bogey!'

In most schools children are punished if they call another child a nasty name. Not in this school. In Greezy Academy the teachers joined in.

'Danny Slimy Bogey!' chuckled the teacher. 'Marvellous! I love it! From now on, that's your name. Right, who wants to sit next to Slimy Bogey? But I have to warn you, he's a thief, so he'll steal your dinner money. And he's half French so he stinks of garlic. Poo!' The teacher waved a hand in front of his face to waft away a non-existent smell.

'Not me!' squealed the children and they pinched their noses and pretended that Danny really did stink of garlic. The big girl pretended to be sick.

'Make him sit at the back,' shouted the big girl when she had finished vomiting. 'Next to the new girl. No one likes her either.'

As one, the whole class turned to stare at the new girl. Danny had not noticed her before; she had been hidden by the big girl's head. The new girl was sitting at the back of the classroom at a table by herself. She was very different to the other children. She could not have been *more* different. Her hair was chestnut brown, not orange, and it was clean and neatly brushed. She was not shouting either or holding her nose or being sick. In fact the new girl was not paying the slightest attention to what was going on in the classroom. Instead she was staring out of the window and wishing she was somewhere else. Wishing she was *anywhere* else.

Straightaway Danny knew he could trust her. It was something Mr Bouygues had told him: *'your enemy's enemy is your friend'*. If Greezians hated the new girl, then he and she were friends and allies. It was logical. Also, the new girl was *really* pretty, although Danny insisted to himself that the way she looked played no part in his decision because that would be shallow.

Quietly Danny sat down in the empty seat beside the new girl and the teacher restarted the lesson. He was showing the children the safe way to open a packet of crisps, whilst driving a car and drinking beer and smoking a cigarette and using a mobile phone. Like all his lessons, this one was destined for disaster because the teacher was far too stupid to teach anyone anything. He only got his job because the headmistress was his mother.

The teacher was sitting on a blue plastic chair in front of the children.

'You have to imagine it's a Porch,' he told them. 'Top of the range, like the one I've got at home. Made in Italy. Now watch carefully and learn from the master. First, you hold the crisps between your legs like this. See?'

The teacher had a large packet of crisps gripped between his thighs.

'And you put your ciggie in your mouth.'

The teacher was using a real cigarette. In most schools cigarettes are banned, even in the staff room. Not in Greezy Academy. In Greezy Academy children were *encouraged* to smoke. There was a cigarette vending machine in the playground and the school football team was sponsored by a tobacco company.

'You hold your beer in your left hand.' The teacher raised his left hand to show the children a pint glass filled to the brim with brown beer. 'And your phone like this.' The teacher wedged his mobile phone between his chins and his shoulder. 'Now this is where it starts getting hard,' he continued. 'So pay attention. It will be in the test at the end of the week.'

The teacher took his right hand off the imaginary steering

wheel of his Porch and wiggled his fingers to demonstrate that he had let go.

'And you steer the car with your knees.' The teacher pressed the top of his knees against where the steering wheel of his Porch would have been if there was a steering wheel.

'I'm Danny,' Danny whispered to the new girl.

'Now you're ready to open your crisps,' said the teacher.

'What's your name?' asked Danny.

The new girl turned her head and looked at him, and Danny realised that he had been wrong to think she was pretty. The new girl was not pretty, she was *beautiful*. Nearly as beautiful as Mrs Bouygues. Except Mrs Bouygues's face was never still. It was always doing something interesting, smiling or frowning or rolling her eyes or laughing. Whereas the new girl's face was set in a blank expression that showed no emotion. It was more like the painted face of a porcelain doll than a human being.

Then it happened. The teacher's phone rang. It was the big girl. She had dialled the teacher on her mobile phone, which she was hiding under her desk.

The surprise was too much for the teacher. He dropped his pint glass into his packet of crisps. His phone slipped from under his chins, bounced twice and landed near the big girl. She silenced the ringing by stamping on the phone and smashing it. Trying to regain control, the teacher steered wildly, swinging the imaginary steering wheel hard left. His blue chair leaned precariously on two legs, balanced for three moments, then toppled over spilling the teacher, beer and soggy crisps across the floor.

'Will that be in the test, sir?' asked the big girl and the other children hooted and jeered and pelted the teacher with screwed-up balls of paper.

Whilst the rest of the class was distracted, the new girl tore a page from her exercise book. She wrote a few words with a silver fountain pen, folded the paper and slid the note across the desk to Danny. Then she turned away from him and looked through the orange glass.

Danny unfolded the paper. It was the first communication he had had with a friendly human being in weeks!

The note was neatly written in navy ink with swirls and loops. There were only six words and the last was in capitals and thickly underlined.

Don't speak to me again. EVER.

Chapter 11

EVERY CLOUD HAS A SILVER LINING

WHATEVER THE SITUATION, Mr Bouygues knew exactly the right thing to say. At least, he thought he knew exactly the right thing to say. Danny and Mrs Bouygues found his little sayings rather annoying. Especially when he repeated them again and again and they were not that funny in the first place.

For instance, when it 'rained cats and dogs', Mr Bouygues said it was 'good weather for ducks' and he put on his wellies and waterproofs and made Danny go for a walk with him. When the oven overheated and burned their dinner, Mr Bouygues did not get cross and kick the oven. He said 'a poor workman blames his tools' and he made slug sushi instead. And when things were going brilliantly and they felt like millionaires, Mr Bouygues said they were 'farting through silk'.

Actually, Danny quite liked 'farting through silk' and he used it himself as often as he could.

And when things were going badly – like the time the Health & Safety Inspector found a rat's nest in the restaurant kitchen and threatened to shut them down – Mr Bouygues said 'every cloud has a silver lining'.

Danny was not sure what Mr Bouygues meant so he looked it up in a library book and discovered it was an old saying that meant no matter how black things seem, never give up hope because there is always a chance of something good, if you keep your mind open to see the opportunity.

Mr Bouygues did; he added rat pie to the menu.

It was late afternoon when Danny saw his silver lining.

It had been a long, tiring day. At morning break the big girl made the other children stand in a circle around Danny and call him names. At lunchtime the headmistress made him stand on the table with a sign round his neck. The sign said:

'Mar naym iz Slarmy Bowgee an mar parints iz thifvs'

The headmistress had written the sign herself, and she was one of cleverest people in Greezy. The teacher could not write at all, not even his own name.

When the other children had finished eating and gone outside to smoke their cigarettes, Danny was allowed to get down from the table and eat their leftover sausages. The sausages were made in the secret kitchen beneath Grimm's Dog Food Factory using meat that was too disgusting to be used in the pies. The sausages were cold and greasy and packed with lumps of gristle that defied chewing, but Danny did not care. It was the best meal he had eaten since he arrived in Greezy and he stuffed his face until the bell rang for the start of the afternoon lessons.

Danny was late for class. As a punishment the teacher made him stand with his nose pressed against the wall and encouraged the other children to throw things at him. Things like books and shoes and rubbers and pencils.

The big girl threw her nappy. The big girl did not have to wear nappies; apart from a small leak when she farted, the big girl was potty trained. And no one made her wear nappies because no one could make the big girl do anything. The big girl wore nappies because she *wanted* to wear them. And she wanted to wear them because she was too lazy to walk to the toilet.

The nappy smacked into the wall beside Danny's face with a wet splat, and stuck there steaming and dripping.

Which was when Danny saw his silver lining.

He did not care if they hated him. The Greezians were horrid and nasty and rude and mean, so he *wanted* them to hate him because if they liked him, that would mean he was horrid and nasty and rude and mean too.

When Danny realised this, he stood up straight and squared his shoulders and dared the children to do their worst.

At once the teacher realised something was wrong. He was tremendously stupid – he had less brains than a frog – but even the dumbest creatures have instincts. So he sent Danny back to his seat beside the new girl, because the game of teasing Danny was only fun if it made him miserable.

The children spotted the change too. They were slightly less stupid than their teacher and they understood what had occurred. Somehow Danny had grown a hard shell and become immune to their insults. So children did the only mean thing that was left for them to do. They ignored Danny and pretended he did not exist.

Which was just fine by Danny Bouygues.

Chapter 12

DETENTION

DANNY LEARNED A lot of useful things that day.
He learned that the big girl's name was Beulah Phlegm
and the teacher – Mr Phlegm – was her dad.

He also learned that everyone – including Mr Phlegm –
was terrified of Beulah. If she did not get her own way in
everything, or if Mr Phlegm dared to suggest that Beulah
had got an answer wrong, she erupted. *Literally.* Her face
swelled and her volcanic pimples popped spewing yellow
rivers. As the eruptions continued, Beulah's chair would
rattle and rock until she burst into a scream that went on
and on…

…until Mr Phlegm changed his question so Beulah's wrong
answer was correct after all.

The bell for the end of school rang just as Mr Phlegm was
changing his question from: 'What is the capital of England?'
to 'Where do you live?', so Beulah's answer of 'Greezy' was
right after all.

'Well done, Beulah,' said Mr Phlegm, mopping his brow
with his tie. It had been a difficult afternoon. Beulah had
erupted five times and Mr Phlegm's head was throbbing. 'You
deserve a special prize for being the cleverest girl in the class.'

Beulah's cheeks flushed. The pimple on her nose swelled.
Her chair began to rattle.

'Errrm!' stuttered Mr Phlegm. He had to act fast. 'Imean-thecleverestgirlintheentireworld!'

The chair stopped rattling and the class breathed a sigh of relief. The eruption was over, for now.

'And as a special prize,' continued Mr Phlegm, 'no homework for you tonight.'

Beulah turned to her classmates and grinned a smug greasy grin. It was the same greasy grin that she had grinned yesterday and the day before and the day before that. And she would grin the same tomorrow because Mr Phlegm always found an excuse not to give Beulah homework.

'And double homework for everyone else,' Mr Phlegm added quickly because prizes were not enough to keep Beulah happy. She had to see her friends being punished too.

'Sir!' moaned the children. But they did not care really. They were too lazy to do their homework and Mr Phlegm was too stupid to mark it.

Mr Phlegm walked through the class handing out worksheets for the children not to do. Until he reached Danny's desk, when he had a nasty idea.

'Where's your homework from yesterday, Slimy Bogey?' asked the teacher.

Danny blinked. He had gotten so used to being ignored that the question caught him unawares.

'Errrm? I wasn't here yesterday, sir. So you didn't give me any homework, Mr Phlegm.' Despite everything that had happened to him, Danny could not help being polite to his teacher. It was the way he had been brought up. Mr Bouygues was very strict about good manners. Mrs Bouygues was less strict because the French believe in being rude when someone has earned it.

Mr Phlegm grinned. 'No excuses!' he roared and he banged on Danny's desk with a clenched fist. 'You're on detention, Slimy Bogey!'

'Hooray!' cheered the rest of the class.

'Double detention!' demanded Beulah, turning around to jeer at Danny. 'That'll teach Slimy Bogey to be a lazy pig!' Beulah had a finger stuffed in her nose on a mining expedition for dried snot. With her cross eyes and a finger poked up her snout Beulah looked stupid beyond compare.

'Treble detention!' shouted the other children.

Mr Phlegm wanted to join in, if he could remember what came after *treble*. He thought it began with the letter *B*. Except *bubruple* did not sound right.

'Quadruple detention, sir?' Danny suggested helpfully, guessing that Mr Phlegm was struggling to find the right word. Mr Bouygues would have been proud. Mrs Bouygues less so.

'Exactly!' bellowed Mr Phlegm and he banged the desk again, so hard that he hurt his hand. 'Quadruple detention for the Slimy Bogey!'

As the other children left for home, they pulled faces at Danny and stuck out their tongues and blew raspberries in his general direction. Beulah flicked a bogey. A little one; she had eaten the rest.

The new girl was the last to go. As she left, the new girl's eyes lingered on Danny sitting alone at the back of the classroom.

Danny was staring out the orange window, so he did not see the new girl looking at him. If he had, he would seen the change in her expression. A smile had been painted on her porcelain mask. Not the mocking, spiteful smile of someone who was enjoying Danny's predicament. It was a hopeful, encouraging sort of smile.

The sort of smile Danny desperately needed.

*****

Danny's punishment was lines.

'My name is Danny Slimy Bogey and my parents are disgusting thieves who deserve to stay in prison forever and ever until they rot. Five thousand times, Slimy Bogey,' sneered Mr Phlegm as he put his feet on his desk and picked up a book. It was Mr Phlegm's favourite book, with pictures and no words and a button to press that made animal noises. Mr Phlegm had never learned to read.

Mr Phlegm pressed the animal noise button.

'*Moo!*' went the book.

Sheeps, thought Mr Phlegm.

Danny got started, writing as fast as he could. He had to finish before 6 o'clock or Aunty Ratbag would make him sleep in the shed. Danny shuddered at the thought of the shed. It was damp and hung with sheets of dusty spiders' webs, and through the gaps in the rough plank floor came the musty smell of rats and the squeakings of their babies.

There was a clock on the wall behind Mr Phlegm. Its hands were moving too fast. Danny glanced up. It was five forty-five and he had only done three thousand five hundred and twenty-seven lines. Which meant he had one thousand four hundred and seventy-three to go. Which meant there was no way he could possibly finish and still be home by 6 o'clock.

Mr Phlegm was also looking at the clock. He was trying to remember what the squiggles meant; he could not read numbers either. He did not need to. His gurgling guts told him it was dinnertime. Which meant it was time to change Beulah's nappy before it leaked.

Mr Phlegm closed his book. He was about to speak when Danny raised his hand.

'Excuse me, Mr Phlegm, sir. Please can I go? I haven't finished, but if I'm not home by 6 o'clock my aunt said she'll lock the door and I'll have to sleep in the shed.'

Mr Phlegm grinned. When Beulah learned of his role in making Danny sleep in a shed, she would be so happy, she might give Mr Phlegm a kiss. And a kiss from Beulah was such a rare treat it was worth being late for supper and mopping the sofa. As Mr Bouygues would say, every cloud has its silver lining.

'Get on with it, Slimy Bogey!' he sneered. 'If you can't do the lines, don't do the crimes!' and he re-opened his picture book and pressed the button.

'*Baaa!*' went the book.

Pigs, thought Mr Phlegm.

Danny's hand was moving across the page in a blur, scribbling desperately. If only he had known that Mr Phlegm could only count up to nine. Before Beulah was born he could count to ten, but baby Beulah had bitten off one of Mr Phlegm fingers – the little finger on his right hand. She had chomped clean through the bone and swallowed his digit. Since then, nine was all Mr Phlegm could manage, unless he took off his shoes and socks. Danny could have stopped at ten lines – or twenty to be safe – and lied and Phlegm would have been none the wiser.

The big hand crept towards to the top of the clock.

'What time is now, Bogey?' asked the teacher

"It's 5.55pm, sir,' replied Danny.

Mr Phlegm stood up. 'Clear off, Bogey. You can finish the rest of the lines tomorrow.'

Chapter 13

A SHORT CUT TO DANGER

D ANNY RACED FROM the classroom. He splashed through
the oily puddle outside the girls' toilet and ran out of
the school, across the playground and down the deserted
road.

It was already night and the streetlamps that should have
lit the way were broken. Beulah's gang had smashed them
with bricks. The moon, half hidden by patches of cloud,
provided a meagre light. The world was shades of darkening
grey.

Danny was a fast sprinter – he had won medals in county
competitions – and although Danny was out of practice, he
flew over the ground, eating up the distance between the
school and Aunty Ratbag's house. The thought of sleeping in
the shed gave his legs the power to carry on.

Until he reached the graveyard.

Danny skidded to a halt. Running was pointless. He could
see Aunty Ratbag's house across the graveyard – he knew it
was hers because there was a light shining in every window
except one - but there was no way he could be home before
6 o'clock. The long route around the outside of the graveyard
past Grimm's Factory would take at least ten minutes. He
was out of time.

Unless he took the short cut *through* the graveyard! The

house was only a hundred metres away. He could be there in fifteen seconds.

Why not? thought Danny. It's only a graveyard at night. What's the worst that can happen?

Danny put a hand on the wrought iron gate. The metal was cold to the touch. The full moon emerged from behind a cloud and lit the path that cut through the middle of the graveyard to the exit directly across the road from Aunty Ratbag's house. But at night the graveyard looked even creepier than it had at dawn. The tombstones leaned closer together and the air was tainted with a foul sweet stench that was neither dog or cat food.

'Don't be a coward,' Danny whispered, saying the words out loud to shame his muscles into action.

He pushed the gate. The hinges whined. Somehow Danny had known they would. He pulled his hands into fists and began to run.

The moon was bathing the graveyard in a silvery glow. Danny was running faster than he ever run before. The sound of his feet pounding on the path echoed back and forth between the ranks of leaning tombstones.

Danny was counting his steps. 30, 40, 50, 60. Then 70 and 80! 'I should be there,' gasped Danny.

100.

120.

150.

Danny glanced over his shoulder. The entrance to the graveyard was far behind him. But Aunty Ratbag's house was even further away than when he had started running.

Danny's lungs were bursting. His legs were shaking from the effort of sprinting. He had to stop.

'How did I get it so wrong?' he panted, swallowing deep lungfuls of bad air.

Then Danny noticed something strange. Aunty Ratbag's house seemed to be shrinking into the distance. The many lights were merging into a single twinkle. Danny looked around him. The tombstones were moving as well. They were no longer crushed tight together. Wide spaces had opened up between them.

The graveyard was growing!

A puff of thin mist blew from behind a tombstone. More puffs followed. They coalesced and thickened into dense swirling fog, a wave of whiteness that crashed in silence over the tombstones. Other waves appeared, joining together until a raging sea of boiling creamy fog was surging up the path.

Danny swung 360 degrees, looking for a way to escape. But the fog was everywhere. Danny was trapped on a shrinking island by a rising tide.

The fog reached Danny's feet. Its touch was damp and chill. It climbed Danny's legs and body, and closed above his head. Danny could not move. He could not breathe. He was drowning!

By some strange science, the fog muffled certain sounds. Other sounds it magnified. In the murk Danny heard strange noises. The dull thump, thump of heavy stones falling onto soft ground. The wet sucking of something pushing itself through clay soil. The sound of steel scraping on stone.

Pairs of dim blue lights appeared in the gloom. There were dozens of them. Dozens of dozens. The lights hovered at the height of a tall man's face, a nose-width apart. And they were coming towards him!

A hand slammed onto Danny's shoulder. Its grip was hard as granite.

'WHAT ARE YOU DOING HERE! ANSWER ME!' It was the gravedigger.

As if by magic, the fog vanished, in a heartbeat evaporating into nothingness. The exit from the graveyard appeared. It was only ten paces away. With the strength of a lunatic, Danny twisted himself free from the gravedigger's stony grasp and fled to his aunt's house.

The gravedigger watched until Danny disappeared from view.

The rag was hanging from the garden tap. As the church clock struck the first *'bong!'* of six o'clock, Danny turned the brass handle. On the second *'bong!'* the tap gurgled. On the third, brown sludge trickled out. On the fourth *'bong!'* Danny splashed sludge on his face. On the fifth, he washed his hands.

On the sixth *'bong!'* Aunty Ratbag opened the kitchen door.

'You're cutting it fine,' she observed as Danny raced up the garden path, drying his hands on the rag. 'I hope you had a good first day at school. Did you make some nice friends?'

Chapter 14

THE GRAVEDIGGER

DANNY WOKE TO the sound of digging.

Shuck!

Thunk!

Shuck!

Thunk!

Danny felt each *shuck!* as if the spade was biting into his body and he shivered at every *thunk!*

Danny crept to the window and peeked out between the bars.

Shuck!

The graveyard was back to its normal size. Danny could see the gate on the other side and, beyond it, his new school. It looked so close.

Thunk!

Last night was just a silly dream, Danny told himself. You imagined it. Graveyards don't grow, you idiot!

Shuck!

'It was a trick of the fog,' he said out loud. 'That's all. People think they see all sorts of strange things in fog. I probably got lost in the murk and ran in a circle, that's why the graveyard seemed too big.'

Then Danny remembered that the fog had appeared *after* the graveyard had started to grow.

Something else was wrong. There was no *thunk!*

Danny felt the familiar electric tingle on the back of his neck. The gravedigger was watching him.

Their eyes met, for half a split second. Then Danny ducked below the window. His ears buzzed. His stomach lurched. He tasted sick in his mouth.

'Pull yourself together,' Danny scolded himself. 'He's just an old man. He can't get you. He's outside, over there, and there are iron bars on the windows (oh thank you Aunty Ratbag for the bars!). What would dad say if he saw you hiding from a harmless old man?'

'And what would mum say?' Mrs Bouygues *never* showed her fear. It was something to do with being French.

Slowly, Danny stood up.

The gravedigger was still staring towards him, holding a spade heaped high with clay soil. His clothes and boots were

smeared with mud. His hair was pure white and so were the whiskers on his chin. And he was massive. In the gravedigger's hands the spade looked like a beach toy, the sort Mr Bouygues used to build sandcastles, whilst Mrs Bouygues was kite surfing. The gravedigger was old, but he was old like a mountain. The gravedigger had the strength of ages. He was worn and battered, and unconquered.

With nod of his grizzled head, the gravedigger gestured towards a hut in a corner of the graveyard. Danny had not noticed the hut before because its camouflage was near perfect. It was almost invisible. Factory filth had stained the hut the exact same colour as the tombstones. A chimney made from rusty dog food tins poked through the tar paper roof.

Danny wolfed his breakfast – burnt toast with a smear of margarine and a glaze of marmalade – wiped crumbs of charcoal from his lips and dashed for the kitchen door.

'Where's my kiss?'

Aunty Ratbag's words stopped Danny in his tracks. His blood drained from his face, leaving his skin as waxy white as any Greezian.

'We got off to a bad start,' purred Aunty Ratbat, her inhuman eyes sparkling. 'I'm sure it was my fault. I'm not a well lady, you see. I'm old and I have a bad heart. The doctor has given me pills, but they make me grumpy and bad tempered. There's nothing I can do about it. Could we begin again, Danny? I do so want us to be friends.'

Even when she was lying Aunty Ratbag could not say *'sorry'*.

Inside his head, Danny heard his father warning him: *'A leopard doesn't change its spots.'* But what if Mr Bouygues was wrong? What if Aunty Ratbag was telling the truth? She was old and loads of old people have dodgy hearts. Strong medicines have lots of unexpected side affects.

Aunty Ratbag was smiling at him. She was so ugly and frail looking Danny could not help feeling sorry for her.

'Friends,' said Danny.

'Friends,' agreed Aunty Ratbag. 'Now how about my kiss?'

Aunty Ratbag offered her cheek for Danny. More than anything Danny wanted not to touch aunt, but he could not see a way out. His toes squirmed inside his shoes as he puckered up and gave Aunty Ratbag's cheek the tiniest peck. It made him feel sick. Her skin was cold and clammy. It was like kissing a frog. The pond variety, not the French sort.

Through her lounge window, Aunty Ratbag watched Danny cross the road, hesitate, then walk into the graveyard. She had enjoyed Danny's obvious suffering when she made him kiss her cheek. Yet, at the same time, his revulsion offended her more than she cared to admit.

'The ungrateful dog!' she hissed. 'Wait until tomorrow. I'll make you suffer for that.'

As she spoke, the postman pushed two envelopes through her letterbox. Aunty Ratbag collected them from the mat. The letters were addressed to Danny. Each bore the postmark of a different prison; HMP Holloway where Mrs Bouygues was gaoled and HMP Wormwood Scrubs where Mr Bouygues was banged up.

Aunty Ratbag chuckled. She knew exactly what she would do with the letters. They would make a lovely addition to the mementoes in her trunk.

*****

The gravedigger's hut was hard to find. It was lost in the maze of leaning stones. Danny had to squeeze between the dirty slabs as he followed the white smoke. At last he arrived and knocked.

'COME IN!'

It was the same hard voice as last night. Except in the daylight the voice was not the least bit scary.

Danny found himself in paradise.

The air was rich with the sounds and odours of a traditional English breakfast sizzling in a frying pan. It was almost like being in Mr Bouygues' kitchen, except dung beetles pop with a CRACK! as they fry and road kill hedgehog has a different smell to cooking bacon. In the background, a radio was playing the same boring news programme Mr Bouygues listened to every morning.

Danny's fears melted.

The gravedigger's stone face cracked into a smile.

'Hello Danny. Take a seat. You'll be hungry, I expect. I don't suppose Mavis Gruntfuttock has given you much to eat.' The gravedigger chuckled. 'She was always a mean old rat bag. She fed your father things that would make a dog puke. Lionel never complained though. He said *'beggars can't be choosers'* and he taught himself to cook. Did you know your dad was a good cook? Not just good. Amazing! Your father could cook anything. I've watched him turn pigs' swill into the finest stew you've ever tasted, right here, in this hut, on this stove.'

The mention of his father made Danny feel uncomfortable. Mr Bouygues had warned him to be careful of strangers. If a stranger offered him a treat Danny had been taught to refuse. The gravedigger seemed to know Mr Bouygues, but he could be lying. Mr Bouygues had never mentioned a man who dug holes for dead people.

The gravedigger offered Danny a sandwich. Thick cut streaky bacon gripped between doorstops of crusty bread spread with salty butter. The hot bacon had melted the butter and oily yellow was leaking through the bread.

Danny hesitated and the gravedigger's smile broadened.

'You'd be helping me if you ate it, Danny. I've cooked too much and it will go to waste otherwise.'

Danny relaxed. *'Helping'* a stranger was completely different to accepting a treat from them. When a stranger asked you for your help it was rude to say no. Mr Bouygues was very strict about that.

Danny *'helped'* the gravedigger with three bacon sandwiches, a bowl of porridge with maple syrup, eight sausages, a fourth bacon sandwich and a cup of the finest hot chocolate Danny had ever tasted.

The gravedigger watched Danny squeegee the last trace of chocolate from the mug with his fingers and lick them clean. 'Do you want some more?'

Danny nodded eagerly and held out his mug. When the gravedigger took it, the mug almost disappeared in his enormous hand.

It was a good hand, thought Danny. A workingman's hand. There was soil under the nails and ingrained into the creases along the sides of fingers thickened by years of hard digging. It looked strong enough to tear whole buildings apart. It was a hand you could trust.

The gravedigger made two fresh mugs of hot chocolate and gave one to Danny.

'I'm sorry if I frightened you yesterday. I thought you were a vandal. Beulah and her gang are always breaking in and smashing stuff.'

Danny shuffled. His chair was suddenly uncomfortable. He did not want to talk about last night.

The gravedigger had other ideas. 'You saw something, didn't you.'

It was a statement, not a question. Danny almost choked on his hot chocolate.

'Don't worry. You're not going mad. Strange things happen in graveyards after dark. Especially this one. The same thing's happened to me too. Lots of times. And your dad. Shall I tell you about it?'

The gravedigger explained.

'This is the oldest cemetery anywhere in England. They've been burying dead folks here since long before they built those dirty pet food factories. Greezy might not look much now, but a thousand ago – long before the Norman conquest and 1066, when the country was ruled by the Anglo Saxons – Greezy was the capital city of England.'

'So Beulah was right!' thought Danny out loud.

The gravedigger gave Danny a puzzled look and carried on with his explanation. 'And the home of great and powerful warrior kings.'

The gravedigger grabbed Danny's attention with his words and told him a story the boy could hardly believe.

It was a strange tale and it took a long time telling and the gravedigger was still talking when, in the distance, Danny heard a church clock strike the hour.

Bong! Bong! Bong! Bong! Bong! Bong! Bong! Bong! Bong!

'It's 9!' gasped Danny jumping up. 'I'm late for school!'

'You'd best be off then,' said the gravedigger. 'But remember this, you're always welcome here, Danny Bouygues. And I'm honoured to be your friend.'

Chapter 15

RETURN TO THE GRAVEYARD

D ANNY HAD A better day at school. The other children ignored him, which he did not mind. The new girl ignored him too, which he did, although he tried to hide it. At lunchtime the headmistress made him stand on a chair with the same sign around his neck. Except today Danny read the sign and when he saw the spelling mistakes he laughed so hard he fell off the chair, which made the headmistress so furious she walked into the wall and broke her only tooth.

When the other children had finished their lunch, Danny ate their leftovers. Today the school canteen had deep-fried Grimm's Beef Twisters, which were ribbon-shaped burgers made with of bits of animal that were too disgusting even for sausages. They were salty, greasy, dangerously unhealthy and strangely delicious.

The afternoon lesson was science. Mr Phlegm was supposed to be teaching his class how to play with fire, except he was not good with matches and he broke most of them. With the last match he set fire to his desk and burned yesterday's homework, reducing it to ashes so he could not mark it. Which, of course, was the real point of the lesson.

Danny got his first detention for laughing when Mr Phlegm set fire to the untidy hedge of bristles that stretched across his forehead from one ear to the other. He got double detention for not doing the double homework Mr Phlegm had not given him on his first day at school. And treble detention for not finishing his lines in yesterday's quadruple detention. And bubruple detention because Mr Phlegm did not like him.

Once again the punishment was writing lines.

'Five thousand lines for each detention,' Bogey,' said Mr Phlegm. 'That's errrm...?'

Mr Phlegm chewed his bottom lip and tried to add up four lots of five thousand. Mr Phlegm had a feeling that nine was the wrong answer. '...a big number.'

Danny started writing.

My name is Slimy Bogey and my parents are vile disgusting thieves who deserve to stay in prison forever and ever until they rot.

My name is Slimy Bogey and my parents are vile disgusting thieves who deserve to stay in prison forever and ever until they rot.

My name is Slimy Bogey and my parents are vile disgusting thieves who deserve to stay in prison for ever and ever until they rot.'

Mr Phlegm was reading his favourite book. He pressed the animal noise button.

'*Woof!*' went the book.

'Cats!' muttered Mr Phlegm.

Danny had filled twenty pages, when he realised he had made a mistake. He had stopped writing: *'My name is Slimy Bogey and my parents are vile disgusting thieves'*. Instead, for the last ten pages he had written: *'My name isn't Slimy Bogey and my parents aren't thieves.'*

The mistake made Danny smile, until he remembered that his parents <u>were</u> thieves and they probably would stay in prison until they rotted. And that he might never see them again.

This was too hard a thought to think, so Danny thought about other things. Like why was he writing stupid lines?

You didn't do anything wrong, Danny told himself. And you definitely don't deserve to be punished by that fat idiot.

Calling Mr Phlegm a *'fat idiot'* felt good, even if he only said the words in his head.

If it feels this good thinking rude words, thought Danny, what would it feel like if I wrote them down on paper?

There was only one way to find out.

'My name is Mr Phlegm,' wrote Danny in his neatest writing. *'and I am a fat idiot and my breath stinks like a dog egg sandwich.'*

Danny wrote that five hundred times. Then he got bored, so he wrote: *'My name is Beulah Phlegm and I have a face like a pig.'*

Danny examined the sentence and crossed out *'pig'* and replaced it with *'piggy's bottom.'* And after *'piggy's bottom'* he added *'and I'm so stupid I can't find my enormous fat bum with both hands.'*

Danny had never written rude things about other people; the very idea had never entered his mind before. Until his parents' arrest, he had not known anyone to be rude about. So Danny did not know how powerful rude words can make you feel.

For the remainder of his bubruple detention Danny wrote ruder and ruder sentences about Mr Phlegm, the headmistress and even Aunty Ratbag. When he ran out of English swear words, he began using the French ones he had overheard Mrs Bouygues say when customers did not leave a tip. Danny did not understand what they meant exactly, but some words are so rude they do not need translating. Just the sound of them is enough.

Danny was so absorbed he did not notice the time.

At 5.56pm Mr Phlegm's belly let out a deep rumbling groan.

'Clear off Slimy Bogey,' sneered Mr Phlegm. 'I don't want you to be late home. I'd be so upset if you had to sleep in the shed!'

Suddenly the rude words did not seem quite so funny. When Mr Phlegm reads them I'll get in the biggest trouble ever! thought Danny. If Beulah reads them, I'm dead!

He did not want to imagine what Aunty Ratbag would do.

Danny stacked the pages into a neat pile, with the good pages – the ones where he had written, *'My name is Slimy Bogey and my parents are vile disgusting thieves who deserve to stay in prison for ever and ever until they rot'* – on top. He put the stack of paper on Mr Phlegm's desk and crossed his fingers.

Danny did not race from the classroom. He did not run across the playground, or sprint through the dark street. He knew it was almost 6 o'clock and Aunty Ratbag would be waiting, but it made no difference because tonight Danny was planning to be late home.

He walked with a heavy tread through the dark deserted street. At the entrance to the graveyard he paused and took a deep breath. On the other side of the graveyard Danny could see the lights of Aunty Ratbag's house and, somewhere inside his head, he heard his father's voice.

'Faint heart never won fair maid.'

It was another of Mr Bouygues' little sayings. It meant if Danny wanted to achieve something that was worth achieving, he had to find the courage to face his fears.

Danny pushed the graveyard gate. Tonight the hinges did not creak. Someone had oiled them.

*****

Danny advanced along the moonlit path until he reached the centre of the graveyard.

An owl hooted. *Twit-twoo!*

Nothing happened, so the owl hooted again and louder. *TWIT-TWOO!*

The church clock began to strike the hour.

Bong!

Danny waited. Any second now, he thought.

Bong!

Any second now…

Bong!

Any second…

Bong!

Nothing happened. Nothing at all.

And suddenly Danny realized he fallen for a trick and that he the greatest idiot in the history of idiots. He was a bigger idiot even than Mr Phlegm because *of course* nothing was going to happen. Danny had been a fool to believe him. It was so obvious. The gravedigger had made up his stupid story because he wanted Danny to sleep in the shed. The gravedigger and Aunty Ratbag were on the same team. They had planned the whole thing between them.

Bong!

As the *'bong!'* echoed around the graveyard Danny understood. The gravedigger was lying about wanting to be Danny's friend. He had tricked him because he hated Danny as much as everyone else in England hated him.

The gravedigger's betrayal was too much. It was the last straw and, finally, Danny's spirit cracked. He could not deny the truth any more. Everything that had gone wrong - being questioned by the police, the lady in the green coat, being sent to live with Aunty Ratbag, Mr Phlegm and Beulah and the new girl who hated him. Everything. It was all his parents' fault! They were thieves, that was the reason why everyone hated him. And if Mr and Mrs Bouygues did not care enough to keep him away from Aunty Ratbag, did that mean that his parents hated him too?

'Why did you do it?' Danny pleaded. 'And why did you get caught?'

It happened on the sixth *'bong!'*

The path stretched. Just a bit. Such a tiny bit that Danny missed it.

Then it happened again and this time Danny couldn't *not* see it. The graveyard was growing.

Slowly at first. Then faster and faster, until the path was slithering away from him like a giant angry writhing snake. Danny watched Aunty Ratbag's house shrink into the distance and its lights merge into a single twinkling point.

The tombstones were moving too. Wide lawns of knee-high grass appeared between them and tall trees erupted from the ground, thrusting their twisting branches into the night sky.

A wisp of mist blew from behind an ancient yew. It spread across grassy lawns, joining with other wisps and thickened into a flood of creamy fog that poured up the path towards him. Danny span around. The fog was closing in from every side. Crested foaming waves of silent white were racing towards him.

Danny was brave when the fog touched his legs. He was scared, but he would not give in to his fear. He was brave when the fog climbed to his waist and up his chest, although he wanted to run. He was brave when the fog closed over his face and he breathed the cold dampness. He was even brave when, hidden in the murk, he heard the sound of tombstones falling.

Thump!

Thump!

Thump!

Thump!

The clay soil sucked as the creatures rose from their graves. They shook clods of wet earth from their feet and scraped their weapons on their own tombstones to wipe away the mud.

Danny heard their moans as they staggered towards him. He heard the clank of their iron weapons and the soft *chink-chink-chink!* of their chain-mail armour. He saw the dim blue lights of their eyes appearing in the fog.

And he stopped being brave.

Danny ran. He ran faster than any child has ever run. He ran faster than any child *will* ever run.

And the eyes followed, keeping pace and there were more of them than Danny could count.

Danny tried to stay on the path, but in the murk he lost his way. He felt tall grass under his feet. Brambles clawed at his legs. Tombstones and trees appeared suddenly blocking his way. Danny darted between them and leapt across open graves. When he stumbled, he rolled and sprang to his feet.

But it was no use. The eyes had won. They were in front of him. They were behind. They were on every side and the eyes were closing in. Danny was trapped.

The creatures staggered towards Danny. As they drew

closer their faces emerged from the fog. But they were not faces. They were…!

Danny stumbled backwards. His legs buckled beneath him. 'No, no!' he begged.

Danny felt a solid wall behind him. He turned and through the murk he saw the outline of a mighty door carved from solid stone.

Danny felt the creatures' breath on his exposed neck. He felt their terrible hands reaching towards him. The door was his only escape. Although he knew the stone door was far too heavy for a boy to open by himself, Danny pushed it anyway.

At his first touch, the stone door swung inwards, silently, on oiled hinges.

'Welcome Danny Bouygues,' boomed a voice. 'I've been waiting for you.'

It was THE KING.

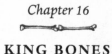

Chapter 16

KING BONES

THE KING WAS seated on a golden throne surrounded by his army. He was dressed in a coat of gilded chainmail that stretched from his neck to below his knees. About his shoulders he wore a silk cloak dyed the colour of ripe plums, richly embroidered with gold and silver thread, and trimmed with ermine. On his head rested a gleaming crown encrusted with rubies and sapphires.

Beside the king stood his huscarls - his bodyguard of loyal knights. Some were armed with a heavy spears. Others leaned on mighty war axes or gripped gleaming broadswords. Each huscarl carried a round shield painted with dragons or sea serpents or wild boars. Iron helmets protected their heads.

The chamber was lit by flaming torches and their flickering light cast queer dancing shadows on the rough-hewn rock walls. In the corners piles of treasure sparkled.

Danny did not see the treasure or the huscarls or their shields and helmets or their sharp weapons. All Danny saw was the king's face and the king's hands and his feet.

They were naked bone, bare of skin and muscle. The king was a skeleton.

So were the huscarls and the other warriors that pressed in behind Danny, forcing him further into the chamber.

'Close the door!' commanded the king and the warriors pushed it shut. The massive stone door closed with a thud that shook the ground. Fine dust fell from cracks in the vaulted ceiling high above.

The king grinned at Danny. At least, Danny thought he was grinning. The king had no face so it was impossible to be sure.

'Bring the boy a seat,' ordered the king and skeleton servants hurried forwards carrying an oaken chair. The chair was too high for Danny to climb, so a skeleton warrior lifted him up. The warrior's bone fingers – cold, hard and pointed as icicles – dug into Danny's soft flesh.

'Thank you,' whispered Danny, politely, although he wished the skeleton had left him alone.

'You're welcome,' breathed the skeleton warrior. The warrior's voice was a hollow hiss, devoid of life and love and warmth and hope. It was the voice of death himself. 'Would you like a cushion?'

A cushion? Even in his craziest wildest dreams Danny had never imagined himself standing in the tomb of a dead Anglo-Saxon king surrounded by his army of skeleton warriors. But if he had imagined himself in such surroundings, Danny was certain the dream would not have included being asked by a skeleton warrior if he wanted a cushion.

Which means I'm not dreaming, thought Danny. This is really happening!

'I'll have a cushion too,' said the king in his huge booming voice and he turned to Danny to explain. 'It's murder sitting on a golden throne when you haven't got a bottom,' he said, solemnly. 'My armour's grinding my bum-bones into dust. I don't know why I wear it.'

Danny was so shocked he forgot his manners and without thinking he blurted out, 'Then why do you wear it?'

The blue lights in the king's eye sockets flashed hot red.

'I mean, why do you wear it, your Majesty?' said Danny quickly, guessing that kings - even dead ones - are touchy about etiquette. Their royal dignity demands that commoners show them the proper respect.

'That's better,' breathed the king and the fire cooled in his skull.

'Firstly,' he continued, smoothing wrinkles in his chainmail. The metal rings tinkled at the touch of the king's bony fingers. 'Because it's expected. And secondly...'

Danny waited, mouth half open. What would the king say?

'...because I've got nothing else to wear. It's what I was buried in. Your children don't think about comfort when they're planting you in your grave. Oh no! It's 'let's dress daddy in his finest suit of armour!''

The king had stopped booming and now he was speaking in a high-pitched squeak. Danny guessed it was the king's impression of his children's voices.

'It's so thoughtless!' boomed the king in his normal voice. 'I mean, would you choose to go to bed in chainmail? Of course not. So why dress daddy in welded iron rings when you're putting him to bed forever? I'd much rather be wearing pyjamas.'

'And socks,' hissed one of the huscarls. 'I really miss socks.'

'And slippers,' hissed another skeleton. 'Slippers would be just the thing on these stone floors. They're freezing. If I wasn't already dead, I'd have caught pneumonia and died ten centuries ago.'

Other skeletons joined in. 'It's alright for you huscarls,' grumbled one. 'At least you're in here with the king. What about us poor souls of the fryd stuck outside?'

From school history lessons, Danny remembered that the fryd were the poorest soldiers in the Anglo Saxon army. They were ordinary peasant farmers who left their fields to fight for their king and returned to the plough as soon as they could.

'When it rains my grave fills up with water,' continued the skeleton whose armour, Danny noticed, was cheap homemade stuff, a sort of padded leather nightie. 'And the worms. The worms! They get everywhere!'

To prove his point, the skeleton plucked a wriggling earthworm from his empty eye socket and threw it on to the stone floor.

'Errrgh!' squawked the huscarls and they leapt back in horror. The skeletons were not exactly scared of worms, but they did not like them. Once a worm has feasted on your flesh, you can never forget or forgive.

'Shut up!' ordered the king crossly. 'For goodness sake! You're supposed to be fearless warriors skilled in the arts of brutal warfare. And you're complaining about worms and socks.'

'And slippers,' muttered one of the skeletons.

'You started it,' whispered the skeleton that lived outside. 'With your *I need a cushion because I haven't got a bottom.*'

But he only whispered the words because a king without a bottom is still a king.

A servant appeared with a plump velvet cushion. The king slipped the cushion inside his armour, between his bones and his grating chainmail.

'That's better,' he sighed. 'Are you comfortable, Danny Bouygues?'

'Very,' said Danny. He had been given a velvet cushion too. Danny's cushion had silver tassels. The king's tassels, Danny noticed, were made of gold. 'Thank you for asking, your Majesty. Errrm? Can I ask another question?'

The king nodded and his golden crown wobbled on his white skull exposing strands of ginger hair. It was exactly the same colour as Mr Phlegm's!

'W-w-w-why did you say you were waiting for me?' stammered Danny. Seeing the king's orange hair had thrown him more off balance than Aunty Ratbag's stool. Were the king and Mr Phlegm related?

'Because we need your help,' said the king. And he explained the what, the why and the how.

It was a sorry tale.

'We're lonely,' moaned the king. 'I miss the queen and my warriors miss their wives. When we were alive they nagged us mercilessly. From dawn to dusk it was *'take your axe off the table'* or *'your stallion has dropped a huge pile of steaming horse apples in the Great Hall'* or *'your spurs have ripped holes in the bed sheets'.'*

The king was doing another impression. This time it was an annoying nasal whine.

The other skeletons nodded in agreement and their iron helmets wobbled on their naked skulls and their teeth rattled in their bony jaws. Their wives had nagged them too.

'But death goes on forever,' continued the king. 'And eventually, after five hundred years, we began to miss them. We even miss the nagging.'

The other skeletons looked sad.

'When our wives died, according to Anglo Saxon law, they should have been buried beside us to share eternity. But our wives were so angry they insisted on being buried elsewhere.'

'Why were they angry?' asked Danny.

'It's stupid really,' said the king with a small cough.

It was a cough that Danny recognised because it was the same small cough that Mr Bouygues coughed when Mrs Bouygues caught him doing something that he did not want to be caught doing. Like playing hide-and-seek with Danny when he was supposed to be unblocking the toilet. The small cough meant the king was embarrassed. And was that a blush of pink on the king's cheekbones?

'It's because of how we died,' mumbled the king, scratching his head and examining the tips of his fingers closely and avoiding looking Danny in the eye.

'It was after a dreadful battle with the Welsh,' he continued, pulling the air where his ear would have been if the worms had not eaten it. 'Did you know that the men of Wales are our worst enemies?'

'You died in battle!' interrupted Danny. 'How exciting.'

'If only we had died in battle!' lamented the king. 'But it was after that. We won the battle and slaughtered the Welshmen. We hacked them into tiny little pieces!' The king's eyes blazed with pleasure as he remembered the slash and hack of ferocious combat with worthy opponents.

Around the chamber the other skeletons murmured excitedly, reliving the cut and thrust and axe-swishing skull-crushing body hewing thrill of battle.

'Anyway,' said the king. 'Slaughtering Welshmen is a messy business and I thought it would be a good idea to take a swim in the river to wash away the blood and gore. The queen said we should take our armour off. But would I listen? Of course I didn't. That's how we drowned. Me and my entire army, because it's a warrior's duty to follow their king, right or wrong.'

'Hear, hear!' cried the king's bodyguard of loyal huscarls and they banged their weapons on their shields. 'Death or glory!'

Danny was not completely sure, but he thought he heard someone at the back of the tomb whisper, 'Stupid old fool!' and some other skeletons respond with stifled giggles.

The king heard the whisper too, but he said nothing. The king and his warriors had lived together in the graveyard for centuries and discipline was breaking down. To avoid outright mutiny, sometimes it was better if the king chose not to hear what his warriors said. Fortunately, choosing not hear was one of the perks of being a king because when a king chooses not to hear or see or smell something, that something never happened.

The king carried on with his tale. 'The queen was furious to be made a widow and she converted to Christianity just to spite me. Until then Greezy was a pagan kingdom and we worshipped the old gods - Woden, Thunor, Frige and Tiw - and we believed in elves and dragons too. We still do, don't we, lads?'

The warriors grunted their agreement.

'When I was in charge, if a Christian monk disturbed my peace with his wishy-washy *'love thy neighbour'* and *'turn the other cheek'* nonsense, my huscarls would bind his arms and legs with leather thongs and throw him into the bog as a sacrifice to Woden!'

The huscarls cheered and banged their weapons against their shields to show approval. A chorus of the rowdier elements of the fryd began to chant: 'Drown the monks! Drown the monks! Drown them in the bog!'

The king continued, his self-confidence restored by his warriors' hearty support. 'But no matter how many missionaries we drowned there were always more of the hair-shirted pests desperate to join their *'Holy Brothers'* in my bog so other Christian fools would call them *'saints'*. Idiots! Then I died and the lousy swine took advantage of the queen's grief. When the next monk arrived, what did the queen do? Did she bind the baldy rascal's arms and toss him off the bridge? No she didn't!'

'Boo!' called some of the warriors. Others cried, 'Shame!' And everyone stamped their feet.

'Instead of spilling his monkish blood, the queen invited the cheeky monk into *my* Great Hall and sat him on *my* throne! She fed him *my* roast swan and *my* honey cakes. And in place of bog water she gave him *my* beer to wet his throat!' The king's eyes glowed crimson at the memory of the insult. 'And whilst he feasted, and his filthy backside dirtied my throne, and his greasy lips polluted my drinking horn, he poisoned the queen's mind with his wicked lies! Before the cock crowed three times, the queen had stopped believing in dragons and trolls, and became a Christian! Woden help us! A Christian! She even built a church and started praying! It's that church with that ruddy bell that torments us with its infernal bonging. And when she died, instead of being buried beside her husband as pagan law demands, the queen was planted there. In a Christian church in hallowed ground! The wives of my warriors are buried with her.'

'The church next to the dog food factory,' hissed the huscarl who liked socks.

'Not the one opposite the cat food factory,' added the skeleton that liked slippers.

'They're buried in a secret chamber deep underground,' said the king, struggling to control his temper. He hated being interrupted when he was telling a story. 'The entrance is hidden behind the heallwahrift showing us riding into the river and drowning.'

'What's a heallwahrift?" asked Danny.

'For Woden's sake!' complained the king. 'Don't they teach you anything nowadays? A heallwahrift is a picture made with coloured threads stitched onto a sheet of woollen cloth. This one's big as a barn door. Our wives made it. It's quite good actually, although they made me look fat and I was never fat.'

This time all the skeletons sniggered, even the loyal huscarls, because in life the king had been a total bloater. He stuffed his face with rib of beef and swan pie washed down with horns of honey mead until his belly bulged over his sword belt and stretched the links of his chainmail.

The sniggering washed around the tomb, growing louder with every circuit. Sniggers became giggles, and giggles turned to sharps snorts of laughter. Until the inevitably happened; one of the huscarls lost control. He tried to stop himself - he clamped a skeletal hand in front of his mouth – but his giggles merely changed direction and escaped through the hole where his nose used to be before the worms ate it. The sound came out like a whistle.

Which set the others off. Guffaws burst out on every side. Bony legs went wobbly at the knee, and huscarls and the common fryd fell against each other, clutching their creaking rib cages and howling. One fearsome knight – who had split a Welshman from crown to crutch with a single swipe of his axe – got the hiccups and dropped his dragon-painted shield, which rolled about the floor in ever decreasing circles before it toppled over with an echoing clang.

'Anyway,' shouted the king, trying desperately to pretend that his army was not laughing at him. It was beyond the king's dignity to admit that half of his army had lost the power to stand. Huscarls and fryd were on their hands and knees, crying dry tears and gasping for breath.

The king had to bellow to be heard above the din. 'Eventually our wives forgave us! But it was too late! The iron key that unlocked the secret chamber below the church had been lost, and the queen and her ladies-in-waiting and my warriors' wives were trapped inside! But at last, after long centuries of searching, the key has been found!'

At once the skeletons stopped laughing. They staggered to their feet, wiped the dry tears from their cheekbones, collected their weapons and shields from the floor, straightened their armour and grew deadly serious.

When the king spoke again, his voice had regained its regal grandeur. 'My raven saw it.' The king clicked his fingers and a bird with a vicious black beak flew across the room and landed on the king's right shoulder. The bird was a skeleton too, except for a few ebony feathers on the wings and tail.

'For centuries my faithful friend kept watch on the mound where my Great Hall used to stand, until the Normans burnt it to the ground.'

The king pronounced 'Normans' like Aunty Ratbag said 'family.'

'Then six months ago, he saw a girl walking with her dog. He saw the girl trip, fall head first into a rabbit hole and, when she came out, she was holding the key!'

'Who was the girl?' asked Danny, hoping that it was not Beulah Phlegm.

'We don't know her name,' admitted the king. 'But you'll recognise her easily enough because she isn't Greezian born and bred. She's a foreigner in these parts, like you Danny.'

It was all the description he needed.

Chapter 17

THE QUEST

THE KING KNEW about Danny's parents. The gravedigger had given him a radio. Mostly, they listened to music – the king was a great fan of disco. His army preferred heavy metal – but in the mornings they listened to news programmes. The king had a keen interest in Royal finery. In life he had plundered rival nations and seized their riches for himself. The fruits of his raiding overflowed from the many chests around the chamber.

'You are the child of thieves, Danny,' said the king. 'So you too shall be a thief and a robber. Your profession in life was determined by your birth, as surely as my heirs were destined to rule and the sons of my huscarls were fated to be warriors, and the children of the fryd were foredoomed to work in pig muck and sweat. You are a natural born thief, Danny. That is why I have brought you here.'

Danny was suddenly uncomfortable.

'I have a quest for you, Danny Bouygues,' continued the king. 'One that will make use of your talents. I want you to find the new girl, break into her house, steal the iron key and bring it to me here. Fulfil this quest, Danny Bouygues, and I will reward you beyond your wildest dreams.' With a dramatic sweep of his arm, the king gestured towards the overflowing chests of gold and jewels.

Danny chewed his lip and thought. He knew that stealing was wrong, like borrowing your father's car and driving it into a duck pond. But stealing was even worse than that, because stealing had a victim beyond tadpoles and water beetles. Stealing hurt *real* people.

Like the old lady who had lived in the house next to the Bouygues' restaurant. One night she was burgled. Thieves broke in, tied her up, ransacked her house and stole everything of value, including her wedding ring. The old lady was so upset she had to move into a retirement home. Three weeks later she was dead.

'Zee awld dear dyed uv a broken art,' Mrs Bouygues had said. 'Zose thifs as goad as mowdered er. Eve eye cadge zem eye wood dwown zem een zee pownd!'

Danny wondered what his mother would do if she discovered that he had broken into someone's house?

Then Danny remembered that Mrs Bouygues was in prison for doing exactly that. Well, almost. The Queen was staying in one of her other palaces on the night of the burglary. But Queen Elizabeth was an old lady. When the Queen heard about the theft of her jewellery she must have felt frightened and vulnerable too.

They're hypocrites, thought Danny and he remembered Mr Bouygues telling him on many occasions that hypocrites were the worst sorts of people and warn him never to believe anything they said. But if his parents were hypocrites did that mean Danny had to doubt everything they had ever told him?

Danny looked at the expectant expressions of the king and his skeleton warriors. He did not want to disappoint them. They needed him and, right now, Danny desperately needed to be needed. But what was he to do? To become a thief or not to become a thief? That was the question.

Danny knew what Mr Bouygues would say: *'Seize the day!'* Which meant don't faff about or you might loose your chance.

But Mr Bouygues would also say: *'Act in haste, repent at leisure.'* Because Mr Bouygues' advice was rarely *'do this or don't do that.'* Nearly always he encouraged Danny to think carefully, trust his instincts and make his own decision.

'Can I sleep on it?'

The king chuckled and addressed his warriors. 'I think we can give him 24 hours, what do you say? The boy's only an apprentice thief who hasn't committed his first solo robbery.'

The king turned to Danny. 'Honest fear is nothing to be ashamed of. I was the same before my first battle. I was up half the night worrying. What if I didn't like killing Welshmen! What if I dropped my sword? What if I was scared witless and soiled my breeks?'

'It's not just that,' Danny lied. 'I don't know how to break into houses. My parents didn't teach me.'

'Then take this,' said the king, and he plucked the little finger from his right hand. He gave the finger to Danny. 'It's a skeleton key. With this you can open any lock in the world. Except the secret door behind the heallwahrift in the church.'

'The church next to the dog food factory,' interrupted the skeleton that liked socks. 'Not the one opposite…'

'HE KNOWS WHICH CHURCH!' The king's eyes blazed and he beat his fists so hard they made dents in the golden armrests of his throne.

Whilst the skeleton army shifted uncomfortably before the king's fury, Danny held the king's little finger up to the flickering torchlight. There were three small bones bound together with threads of shrivelled sinew. It looked like a dry twig, stripped of its bark and bleached by age.

'It uses pagan magic,' explained the king. 'My finger is enchanted with the power of the god Loki, the brother of the great Woden. As I am sure you know, pagan magic doesn't work in a Christian Church. That is why we *must* have the iron key the foreign girl has found.'

'Why didn't you use the skeleton key yourself to break into the foreign girl's house?' asked Danny.

'Because we are warriors not common thieves,' said the king proudly, although the heaps of treasure in the shadows of his tomb were the fruits of plundering many rival king-doms. 'Stealing is beneath us. Also, the girl has a dog…'

'Surely you're not scared of dogs!' gasped Danny in disbelief.

The king coughed and pulled the air where his ear used to be. 'I'm not scared, but my warriors are a little intimidated. And before you mock, Danny Bouygues, remember that one day you will be a skeleton too. The undead fear nothing, but we cannot fight dogs. When they see our bones, dogs go mad with lust. And the girl's pet isn't some yapping pooch. He is a pure-blooded Celtic dog of war, tall as a pony and swift as the north wind, with a pedigree that reaches back to the mighty hound of Codswallop ap Bedpan, the king of the Welshmen. Many of my warriors lost hands and limbs to that fell beast.'

A score of skeletons held up arms with missing hands snapped off below or above the elbow. One displayed a leg bitten clean through at the thigh.

'No skeleton can face that dog. The beast has the jaws of

120

the Red Dragon of Gwynedd! Although, I'm sure he won't bite you, Danny. Probably,' the king added, unconvincingly.

It was time for Danny to leave. Skeleton warriors opened the door of the king's tomb and the fog rolled in.

Danny bowed low to the king and he was about to go when he remembered he did not know the king's name.

'What should I call you?' he asked.

The king got up from his golden throne and stretched out his skeleton arms and filled his lung-less chest with air.

'BONES!' he shouted. 'KING BONES!'

Chapter 18

DANNY'S BRILLIANT IDEA

AUNTY RATBAG WAS waiting for him and she was furious. She had been planning to be nice. She had found an old newspaper that Danny could use as a pillow and cooked a special soup with an extra stalk of frozen broccoli and water from the hot tap. But the thoughtless boy had ruined everything by arriving home after 6 o'clock. Because *The Rules* were *the rules* and Aunty Ratbag stuck to them whether she liked it or not.

'You selfish brat!' she scolded him, leaning far out of her bedroom window. 'I warned you not to be late! You can forget about supper and sleeping in your bedroom! It's the shed for you tonight!' And she slammed the window shut and drew the curtains. They were very ugly curtains. Probably the ugliest in the entire world.

With his Aunt's curses stinging his ears, Danny trudged down the narrow passageway. As he emerged into a grim garden that was already littered with clutches of fresh eggs, the last gristled nugget of Beef Twister dissolved in his belly and Danny's empty guts emitted a strangulated groan.

Danny stepped close to the kitchen door and peered through oranged glass. Aunty Ratbag had left his bowl at the far end of the table. In the hot water the frozen stalks of broccoli were melting into vegetable slurry.

Danny's stomach groaned again. He had stuffed it with worse meals and survived. And besides, there was nothing else on the menu. In case Aunty Ratbag had made a mistake, Danny turned the handle and pushed gently. But the door did not budge.

With only an ache to fill his belly, Danny zigzagged between the dog eggs to reach the garden shed. Inside, he ducked below the dusty sheets of spiders' webs and made his bed on the hard floor. As he squirmed to find the least uncomfortable position, the planks creaked disturbing rats whose squeaking awoke memories of Mr Bouygues' rat pie, which set his stomach growling again.

Danny's body was cold and tired, but his mind was sharp. Too much had happened to sleep and he had decision to make.

As well as teaching her son to read and write in a dozen languages, Mrs Bouygues had taught Danny how to think logically.

'*Thay eez o'wayz adleez toe sighdz toe ev'ree arrg-yew-mont,*' Mrs Bouygues had told him. '*Ewe av toe theenk abou'd zem bowf bee'foe ewe mayk yo diz-iz-yonn.*'

What were the two sides in this *arrg-yew-mont*, pondered Danny?

If he did as King Bones asked and burgled the new girl's house and stole the key, he would be '*helping*' the king, which was good. Also, King Bones had promised to reward him beyond his wildest dreams. And Danny's dreams were pretty wild. He could use the treasure to hire a brilliant lawyer to free his parents. And, if that did not work, he could run away and start a new life far away from Greezy and Aunty Ratbag.

On the other hand, if he did *not* steal the key, King Bones would call him a coward and Danny would spend the rest of his life cleaning Aunty Ratbag's windows and filling shopping bags with dog eggs.

So why are you hesitating?

Danny knew the reason well enough: he did not want to become a thief. His parents were hypocrites who could not be trusted, but that did not mean that *everything* they said was wrong. Danny had known the old lady in the village, the one who was burgled. She was a bit crazy. Every Christmas she gave him an Easter egg, and at Easter she gave him a box of mince pies. She bought them cheap after the proper holiday, so her presents were always mouldy, but she meant well. When the old lady was robbed Danny saw with his own eyes how she shrivelled up.

Could I do that to the new girl? He wondered. Even if she was horrid and deserved it?

Danny shook his head and the dream of escaping Aunty Ratbag began to fade. Except Danny did not want the dream to disappear and his brain began to search for a third side to the *arrg-yew-mont* that would free him to steal the key without feeling guilty.

Then Danny had a brilliant idea.

What if I take the iron key and rescue the queen, then return it to the new girl's house *before* she realises the key's missing? That is not stealing. It's borrowing! And borrowing is not against the law. In fact, logically, it's sharing and sharing is good.

Danny had an uncomfortable feeling there might be a fourth side to this argument, so he switched to thinking about practical matters. How he was going to break into the new girl's house? Then Danny remembered the skeleton key.

King Bones had said his little finger could open any lock in the world.

Danny held the skeleton key close to his face. There was just enough moonlight creeping into the shed window to see it. The finger did not look the least bit key-ish. How did it work? He would have to practice before he robbed the new girl. But practice on what?

Danny's stomach had the answer.

Of course! He could test the skeleton key by using it to breaking into Aunty Ratbag's kitchen. That way, he could 'kill two birds with one stone', because he could also take some food.

The moon was hidden behind a cloud. Danny was grateful for the dark. It hid his embarrassment as he held the skeleton key up to the brass lock of Aunty Ratbag's kitchen door. King Bones' little finger was entirely the wrong shape to fit into the zigzag keyhole. He felt foolish for even trying.

Then the magic happened. The king's finger pulsed with a soft blue light and, before Danny's disbelieving eyes, the three small bones fused together to become a single piece. A piece that twitched and trembled and…

…changed shape!

The bones stretched and flattened. From the tip, strange threads appeared that twisted into jagged teeth, until the king's little finger was unmistakably a key. A very large key. Unmistakably the wrong sort of key. The sort of key that opens a castle gate, not the kitchen door of an ordinary house.

The skeleton key appeared to know that it had made a mistake and it changed into a different shaped key. Different, but equally wrong. It tried again and again, twisting and changing, faster and faster, until it was a whizzing blur, transforming into tens and hundreds of different shaped and sized keys. Tiny keys to wind up pocket watches. Giant keys to open dungeons. Even the most secret key of all. The key that every McSweeny dreams of owning. The key that opens the big safe at the Bank of England.

Danny was beginning to think that the skeleton key must be broken, when it stopped in the shape of an ordinary key. The sort of key that might open an ordinary kitchen door.

With an unsteady hand, Danny slipped the skeleton key into the zigzag hole. The key went in smooth as a hot knife through warm milk chocolate. It was a perfect fit.

Danny turned the key and…

Click!

A soft push and the kitchen door swung wide open.

Danny took a small step into a dark place. He knew that he could not risk switching on the light. If Aunty Ratbag caught him the punishment was displayed above the kitchen table: *'Rule 10. INSTANT DEATH.'*

Danny's eyes became accustomed to the gloom. Cautiously he navigated around the table and chairs. One bump, one tiny accident and Aunty Ratbag would pounce. She was in the next room. He could hear the television and the *clunk!* of what sounded like a stapler.

Danny did not touch the broccoli soup; Aunty Ratbag would know if he ate that. Instead he searched through the kitchen cupboards, taking things from boxes that were already open and never enough to be noticed. Two slices of bread, a few biscuits from different packets and one Belgian chocolate. It was a white chocolate filled with hazelnut praline and topped with a crystallised violet. From the fridge he took a single slice of ham and a spoonful of pickle.

Danny left as quietly as he had come, softly closing the kitchen door behind him with barely a sound.

That was so easy, Danny thought. King Bones was right. I am a natural born thief. I was in and out in less than sixty seconds and I didn't leave a crumb of evidence!

Danny took a bite from his ham and pickle sandwich, and chewed and swallowed. It was the perfect crime. Even Ice Pick McSweeny would have been impressed. Except for one tiny detail.

Danny had closed the kitchen door, but forgotten to re-lock it.

Chapter 19

A GRAVE WARNING

DANNY SKIPPED BREAKFAST with Aunty Ratbag and raced to the gravedigger's hut. He did not wait for an invitation. He burst in and found the gravedigger making pancakes. There was a choice of homemade rhubarb jam or caramel sauce with bananas. Danny had four of each, and a bacon sandwich.

When he had finished stuffing, over a steaming mug of hot chocolate (that did not taste quite as good as yesterday's) Danny told the gravedigger every detail about his meeting with King Bones and the king's quest.

'He wants me to steal an old key and rescue his queen from a secret chamber under the church!'

Danny was so electrified he did not notice the frown spreading across the gravedigger's granite face.

'Obviously, I can't steal it…' Danny blurted.

The gravedigger's frown subsided.

'…because stealing is against the law. And it's wrong too.'

Danny told the gravedigger about the old lady in the village and the gravedigger's frown relaxed into a smile.

'But I've thought of a brilliant solution! After I've rescued the queen, I'm going to put the key back! So I'm *borrowing* the key, not stealing it!'

The frown had returned to the gravedigger's face.

'What do you think?' Danny paused, eager for the gravedigger to congratulate him. Only then did he notice the sadness in the gravedigger's eyes.

Slowly, heavily, the gravedigger shook his head. 'I'm sorry, Danny. I've made a terrible mistake. I didn't know the key was already found. King Bones kept that news to himself. I thought he would ask for your help searching for it, like your father used to. Looking for that key stopped Lionel from going mad. When things got too bad at home or school, he bunked off lessons and spent hours searching. King Bones shouldn't have asked you to steal it. If I had known that was his plan, I would never have introduced you.'

'But you did,' said Danny. 'And you were right to. Helping King Bones will help *me*. I *want* to do this.'

The gravedigger shook his head again. 'The road to Hell is paved with good intentions, Danny,' he warned gravely in his gravelly voice. It was the sort of thing Danny's father might have said and it was even more annoying coming from the gravedigger. 'Stealing an old key to help King Bones sounds like a little thing when you say it. But it's the first step into a life of crime.'

The gravedigger stirred his hot chocolate, tapped the teaspoon on the rim and placed the spoon on the table pointing at Danny.

'You're standing at the top of a slippery slope, Danny boy. Most people are expecting you to stumble and fall. More than a few would gladly give you a push. Don't give them the satisfaction. If you do this – if you break into the new girl's house – next time thieving won't be so hard. Every time you steal it gets easier. Trust me, I know. And once you start you can't stop. You'll be smashing into old folks' houses, tying up grannies and stealing their life savings.'

Danny was flabbergasted.

'I'm not robbing old grannies! Weren't you listening? I'm going to return the key after I've rescued the queen, so it's *borrowing*, not *stealing*.'

The gravedigger raised a craggy eyebrow. 'Breaking into someone's house and taking stuff without asking doesn't sound like borrowing to me. That's a bad lawyer's excuse. It's been tried a hundred times in court and it never works. And what if you get caught? Have you thought of that? It's not fair, Danny, but the police won't give *you* a second chance, not after what your parents did. They'll throw the book at you.'

The gravedigger took a long sip of hot chocolate and chose his next words with care.

'If you get nicked, the police will fit you up for every crime in Greezy, including some that haven't happened yet. When the newspapers hear about it they'll go crazy. They'll say *'the fruit doesn't fall far from the tree'* and demand you get the harshest sentence. If you're caught stealing, Danny, just once, you'll spend the rest of your life looking through prison bars. Take it from me, that's not a pleasant view.'

Danny could not believe his ears. The gravedigger was supposed to praise his brilliant plan, not pull it apart.

Danny's disbelief turned to anger and he jumped to his feet, knocking his chair over.

'You said you wanted to be my friend. But a real friend would know that I'd never steal anything. And if I did steal something, that I'd get away with it. Like last night when I broke into Aunty Ratbag's house and...'

The savoury memory of last night's ham and pickle sandwich stuck in his throat. For an unpleasant second Danny
wondered if the gravedigger was right. He had already
burgled an old lady and enjoyed doing it.

The second passed. Of course he isn't right! He's just a
stupid old man in a rubbish town with a rubbish job. All he
knows is digging holes and planting dead bodies! He doesn't
understand what I've been through.

Danny stormed from the hut. Then he remembered his
manners and returned and said: 'Thank you for breakfast,
Mister Gravedigger. I enjoyed it very much indeed.'

Although his words were polite, the tone of Danny's voice
made it crystal clear he was not the least bit grateful. It was a
trick he had learned from his mother.

Chapter 20

SHOPLIFTING

DANNY MARCHED BETWEEN the gravestones with no idea where he was going. He had been hoping to spend the day hiding in the gravedigger's hut. His plan – devised the previous night after his raid on Aunty Ratbag's kitchen - was to bunk off school. Mr Phlegm was bound to put him in detention and, today, Danny had to leave on time so he could follow the new girl to find where she lived. The gravedigger's hut was the perfect place for lying low until school ended. In fact, it was the *only* safe place that Danny could think of.

Danny glanced over his shoulder hoping to see the gravedigger chasing after him. But the gravedigger was nowhere in sight.

Drat him, thought Danny. I don't need his or anyone's help. I can do this by myself.

He was in such a fury he did not realise where his legs were taking him, until he almost collided with the pimply gargoyle that was guarding the school gates. Just in time, Danny came to his senses and ducked behind a hulk of rusted metal propped on four deflated tyres. It was Mr Phlegm's car. He had parked it there five years before and forgotten where he had left it.

Danny peered through oranged windows and between the stripes of dried bird poop and spied on Beulah. She was absorbed in party bucket of Beef Twisters, crunching the tough knuckles of gristle with the placid concentration of a bull eating clover in a meadow. Avoiding Beulah was another reason Danny had decided to bunk off school. No matter how peaceful they seem, bulls are always dangerous.

The school bell rang and Beulah dropped the empty bucket on to the pavement. She wiped her greasy face with her hands and her greasy hands on her shirt, farted fruitily and squelched across the playground to begin another day of bullying. Danny departed in the opposite direction.

Like most children, Danny had often dreamed of bunking off school, especially during double Maths lessons on hot July afternoons. The reality was less exciting. In his dream Danny explored woodlands with friends building camps and damming streams. But there were no woods in Greezy and the only streams were already dammed with supermarket trolleys and trash, and the water was thick green poison. Danny had nowhere to go, nothing to do and no one to do nothing with. Without money he could not go to a café and he was uncomfortable wandering through the streets. The Greezians spotted him for an outsider and they did not try to hide their dislike. Eventually he found a deserted playground. Beulah's gang had been there before. The swings and the slide were broken wrecks. The climbing frame was a mess of twisted metal and melted plastic. And the grass was speckled with toadstools and dog eggs.

It began to drizzle.

Danny sat on a bench and waited, listening to the church clock striking the hour. Ten o'clock, eleven, twelve.

At one o'clock the drizzle turned into rain.

You idiot, Danny told himself. Although he refused to regret arguing with the gravedigger, bunking off school had been a stupid mistake. He should have waited until after lunch and then skipped off with a belly full of sausages.

Danny was toying with the thought of chewing King Bone's finger – the threads of dried sinew might taste of something – when he heard the jangling ringing of shop bell. The exterior of the shop was so encrusted with brown filth stains Danny had not noticed it before.

An idea popped into Danny's head and, once the idea had popped in, it would not pop out.

I'll just have a look, Danny lied to himself. There's no harm in looking.

The bell jangled as Danny entered the shop, alerting the shopkeeper who was sitting behind the counter guarding the till. Danny smiled feebly, hoping his smile did not look as fake as it felt. The shopkeeper did not reply. He was one of the cross-eyed Greezians and Danny was not sure if the shop-keeper had even seen him.

There were three aisles in the shop with tiers of shelves stacked with tins and packets. Danny strolled up the middle aisle, whistling tunelessly, and stopping now and then to lift items from the shelves and read the labels. And all the time he was moving further from the shopkeeper.

A chiller cabinet stretched across the back wall of the shop. The open fridge was supposed to keep the milk and cheese and cooked meats cool and fresh, but the motor was broken. In the absence of cold, the milk had turned sour, the cooked meats were green, and the cheese was full of red worms.

On a shelf next to the wriggling cheddar, Danny spotted a

packet of Grimm's Scotch eggs. The memory of Mr Bouygues' Scotch eggs set his mouth watering.

Danny glanced over his shoulder. Tall shelves blocked Danny's view of the shopkeeper. And if he could not see the shopkeeper, the shopkeeper could not see him either.

I'll just read the list of ingredients, Danny told himself as he lifted the packet of Scotch eggs from the shelf.

His heart was thumping in his chest. And the idea inside his head was whispering temptations. 'There's nothing wrong stealing a few Scotch eggs if you're starving. Anyway, you need to practise if you're going to break into the new girl's house.'

Danny hesitated.

'Go on!' hissed the idea. 'No one can see you.'

Danny dropped the packet of Scotch eggs into his jacket pocket.

Then he saw the mirrors.

The ceiling of the shop was covered with mirrors of every shape and size: rear view mirrors taken from cars and huge wing mirrors stolen from lorries; mirrored doors from bathroom cabinets; tiny mirrors that ladies use to fix their makeup; and the even tinier mirrors that dentists use to examine teeth. Above the chiller cabinet, a mirror ball was suspended on a chain. Without leaving the counter, the shopkeeper was watching Danny in a thousand reflections.

'Doris,' he growled, clearing his nose and spitting on the floor. 'We've got another one.'

'Shoplifter?' came a voice.

'Yeah. A school boy.'

Reflected in the mirrors, Danny watched Doris – the shopkeeper's wife - emerge from the stockroom.

'Where is he?' she asked, her pale cross-eyes searching the mirrors.

'By the chiller cabinet,' breathed the shopkeeper as he slid off his stool.

'Scotch eggs, I expect,' said Doris. 'I'll cut him off and you catch the brat when he tries to leg it.'

There was no chance of that happening. Danny's legs were refusing to obey his brain. Danny could only watch in the myriad of mirrors as the shopkeeper and Doris advanced towards him.

As the hunters closed on their prey, Danny smelt Doris' vile smoker's breath and the viler stink of her feet. He saw the shopkeeper's grin broaden, revealing broken rows of rotting teeth. Reflected in the mirrors Danny saw a thousand hands reaching out, ready to grab him from every direction.

Doris pounced...

...and missed!

She was not even close. There were so many mirrors, each reflecting the reflections of other mirrors, that Doris and the shopkeeper had no idea where they were, let alone where Danny was standing. Viewed through the mirrors, the tiny three-aisled shop had become a multi-dimensional maze, and the cross-eyed hunters were lost within it.

The shopkeeper snatched at Danny's reflection and punched a pyramid of baked bean tins. Doris tripped on a rolling tin and barged head first into her husband, who fell backwards into a display Grimm's Finest Self-Raising Flour, releasing a cloud of powdered horse bones.

Danny seized his chance. He tore his eyes away from the mirrors and, instantly, the maze became a cramped, untidy, three-aisled shop. He took the Scotch eggs from his pocket and put them back into the chiller cabinet.

'I've just remembered,' he said, lamely. 'I forgot my money. I'll fetch my wallet and come back later.' Danny stepped over Doris and her horse-floured husband and fled.

Outside, on the pavement, Danny could not have felt guiltier if he *had* stolen the Scotch eggs. Or more alive! *Almost* shoplifting was the most frightening thing he had ever done. And the most exciting.

Danny did not realise it, but he had taken the next step on the slippery slope. And the gravedigger was right. It did get easier.

Chapter 21

THE NEW GIRL'S HOUSE

A T PRECISELY 3.30pm, Danny was crouching behind Mr
Phlegm's car waiting for the school bell to ring.

Beulah was first out of school, followed by her gang of creeps
and toadies. She positioned herself by the gates where she could
bully the teachers and rob the children as they left. Danny
watched Beulah take sweets from the youngest students and
empty their bags into dirty puddles, and bounce up and down
on her maths teacher's bicycle until the wheels bent. Her gang
sniggered whilst the teacher begged and sobbed.

The new girl was the last to leave. She had hidden in the
toilets, waiting for Beulah and her gang to move away. She
did not care about her schoolbooks, but Beulah had other
nasty tricks. It took hours to clean her hair when Beulah used
it as a tissue.

The new girl crossed the street and walked past Grimm's
and the queue of lorries filled with weary ingredients patiently
waiting for their turn in the mincing machines. She passed an
old church and kept walking until she reached the far side of
town, where Mr Grimm and Mr Slugg and the other rich
Greezians lived. The houses were bigger here, much bigger,
and further apart with large with large gardens filled with
leafy shrubs and trees. And the air was almost fresh, with only
the faintest whiff of pet food.

Danny followed from a distance, keeping out of sight.

The new girl lived in the largest, most imposing house. The house was covered in glossy green ivy and half hidden from the road by holy trees. The entrance to the gravel driveway was guarded by stone eagles that stood on top of tall brick pillars. The eagles' wings were outstretched and their hooked beaks were open as if they had been petrified mid-screech. Rabbits were clutched in their granite talons.

The new girl reached the red front door and stopped.

Danny jumped behind a brick pillar. He counted to ten and peeked. The new girl had disappeared. Danny ran up the driveway, his feet crunching on the gravel.

Suddenly the red door opened. Danny leapt into the holly bushes and crouched. Just in time, before the new girl emerged. In her small hand the new girl was holding a thick leather leash. And at the end of the leash was a dog.

Danny had never imagined that such a beast could exist. It was more like a grizzly bear than a dog, but with larger jaws and longer teeth.

The dog sniffed the air and fixed its eyes on the exact spot where Danny was hiding. With twitching lips, the dog growled a low rumble that Danny could feel through his feet. Holly leaves quivered.

'Shush!' commanded the new girl.

The dog obeyed instantly, although its gaze never shifted from the shrubbery.

'I know why you're grumpy,' she said. 'You've been locked up all day. You just need a good long run. Come on!'

The new girl tugged the lead and the dog trotted beside her, down the gravel drive and between the stone eagles. Strings of gluey saliva dripped from its jaws and collected gravel.

Danny waited until the pair had disappeared from view, counted to sixty to be sure, and then ran to the front door. He took the skeleton key from his pocket and held it close to the lock. The bones pulsed with a blue light and changed shape into an ordinary sort of key.

Danny slipped it into the lock.

Click! The door opened.

Inside, the house was more like a museum than a place where people lived. The walls were panelled with dark wood. The floor was tiled in black and white checks, and somewhere a grandfather clock tock-ticked. Greek vases and busts of Roman emperors stood on tall plinths in every corner and in niches in the wood panelled walls. The air smelt of wax polish and old money.

Fixed to the wall above the marble fireplace was a life-size oil painting of a cruel-faced man and a crueller woman. And, standing apart from the adults, as if the grown ups resented her presence in their picture, was the new girl, who looked nothing like either of her parents. The man was oddly familiar. Danny wondered if he might have seen the man in the Bouygues' restaurant arguing with his mum?

There was no time think about that now and Danny ran upstairs to find the new girl's bedroom. He was sure the key would be there.

The first floor was brighter. There were more windows and the walls were painted white. But the bedrooms had the same museum feeling. They were too tidy and the beds were wrinkle-free.

The new girl's bedroom was on the second floor and, as Mr Bouygues would say, she was farting through silk. Her bedroom was the *whole* of the second floor. Danny could not help feeling jealous. The new girl had her own indoor bathroom, with strawberry-scented shower gel and fluffy towels warming on a towel rail.

Danny began to search, carefully at first. When he picked up a vase to look inside, he put it back exactly where it had been. He checked the desk draws without moving a pencil. He patted the pockets of coats and jackets, and looked under the bed. But the key was nowhere to be found.

'Why have you got so much stuff?' cursed Danny. 'Nobody needs this much junk, do they?'

The time for being careful had passed and Danny began to throw the new girl's things into a heap in the middle of the room. Once he started he could not stop. He swept books off the shelves and ripped the new girl's designer dresses from their coat hangers.

He did not mean to smash the glass animals. It was an accident. The delicate ornaments were on a shelf above the new girl's bed where he could not see them. Breaking them was an accident

The sound of shattering glass stopped him dead. For ten seconds Danny's future hung in the balance.

He could have stepped off the slippery slope, left the girl's room and gone back to Aunty Ratbag's house. In a few days, Aunty Ratbag would have crushed his spirit and reduced Danny to a living zombie. In time, the Greezians would have forgotten about his criminal parents and the zombie Danny would have become indistinguishable from the native population. When he left Greezy Academy, Danny would have got a job at Grimm's turning ponies into pies. Later he would have married Beulah Phlegm and produced a brood of pimply, cross-eyed, foul-mouthed brats.

Luckily, smashing felt fantastic!

Rage grabbed hold of Danny. The new girl deserves it, he told himself, and he began to break everything. He pulled the heads off dolls, and ripped her toy bears apart and flung the stuffing in the air. He tore pictures from the walls, smashed their frames and stamped on the pieces, grinding splinters of glass into the carpet. Searching for the key was a thin excuse that just about covered tearing her toys apart. There was no justification for squeezing shower gel over the mess.

When rage released its grip the room was utterly destroyed. And Danny still had not found the key. There was only one place he had not looked: the chest of drawers beside the new girl's bed.

In the first drawer Danny found the new girl's school uniform, ironed and neatly folded. Danny emptied it onto the floor. Her sport's kit and swimming things were in the next drawer. Danny stretched the rubber strap of the new girl's goggles until it snapped.

There was one last drawer. It was full of coloured knickers. Danny blushed and began to close the drawer when he realised a knicker draw was the perfect hiding place. No thief would think of searching there.

Danny raised the drawer high above his head and emptied it. Knickers fluttered down like autumn leaves. But there was still no key.

As the last pair of knickers settled on the carpet, a waft of air disturbed the curtains. The floorboards creaked. And Danny felt a new sensation on the back of his neck; the hot moist meaty panting breath of a large dog.

Chapter 22

THE SMOKING GUN, PART ONE

A T 3.17pm precisely, Aunty Ratbag left her house and slammed the front door and began closing the deadlocks with brass keys. Home security was essential in Greezy. The town was full of crooks and some of them were stupid enough to break into Aunty Ratbag's house. Over the years she had caught a dozen burglars red-handed and there was no space beneath her shed to hide another one.

Whilst their mistress double-checked, her dogs waited patiently, shivering in their naked mottled skins, with their silly fluffy tails tucked between their legs to keep their tummies warm.

Satisfied that her house was secure, Aunty Ratbag stomped down the garden path and crossed the road in quick strides. When she reached the entrance to the graveyard she stopped. She was going to Danny's school. That was why she was taking her dogs because, whatever the occasion, Aunty Ratbag knew exactly the *wrong* thing to do and she enjoyed doing it immensely. Dogs were forbidden in Greezy Academy in case they fouled in the classrooms, so of course Aunty Ratbag had brought her pets. She had also salted the dogs' breakfasts to ensure they overfilled their bellies with water. For seven hours she ignored their desperate pleas to use the garden. The ugly creatures were about to pop. When they moved they sloshed. Every step was an agony, but they could not wee a single drop without Aunty Ratbag's permission.

Aunty Ratbag observed the dull school buildings on the far side of the graveyard. Dare she take the direct route?

Aunty Ratbag was not scared of the gravedigger. Not *exactly*. She was scared because the gravedigger *wasn't* scared of her. Because if one person could learn to overcome their fear, so might others. The thought was enough to freeze the glass in her eyeballs.

All afternoon Aunty Ratbag had spied on the gravedigger though her net curtains, waiting until the old man stopped for his afternoon tea break. When she saw him climb from his hole, she put on coat and called her dogs to heel. But now, standing by the graveyard gate, she was having second thoughts. What if the gravedigger brought his mug of tea outside?

'Blast the dratted man!' she cursed.

And she kicked the closest dog in the direction of Slugg's.

Chapter 23

A GRAVE MISTAKE

DEEP IN THE graveyard, hidden from the outside world by leaning walls of lichened tombstones, the gravedigger was working. Digging was a slow wearisome business because the earth was full of ancient bones and iron tools of warfare, and the gravedigger took great care not to smash them with his spade. He knew they were needed.

The gravedigger exposed a skull and bent to lift it, putting his fingers into the empty eye sockets and nose hole as if it was a bowling ball. The skull came free from the clinging clay with a wet *shwuck*! and he placed it on top of the high heap of bones beside the open grave.

Then he saw the bright coin clamped between the skull's long teeth.

The gravedigger knew about treasure. King Bones' warriors were buried with the loot they had plundered from Wales and every grave was a gold mine. The gravedigger eased the coin from the skull's bite and tested it with his own teeth. The softer the metal the purer the gold. And this was the finest gold he had ever tasted!

The gravedigger polished the coin on his sleeve to make it gleam and revealed the face of a Celtic prince who had died a thousand years before King Bone's ancestors had crossed the North Sea to settle in Greezy. The gravedigger had unearthed many hoards, but this was the true rarity. A museum would pay a king's fortune to acquire it. A private collector would give him five times as much. With this one coin he could buy a yacht and sail away from Greezy to start a new life on a tropical island. With a handful of coins he could buy the whole island.

The urge to drop the gold in his pocket was irresistible.

'*Almost* irresistible,' the gravedigger chuckled and he gave the skull a friendly wink.

Without moving a twitch, the skull winked back.

It was a game the warriors played. They knew about the gravedigger's past and they liked to tease and tempt his resolution.

The gravedigger refixed the coin between the skull's teeth and clambered out of the half-dug grave. It was 3.15pm precisely and time for his afternoon tea break. The gravedig-

ger wended between tombstones to his hut and whilst he waited for the kettle to boil, the gravedigger's mind wandered back to the events of that morning and his argument with Danny.

Should I have run after the boy and explained? he asked himself.

He almost had and he was sick with worry in case he had made another mistake. Danny had said nothing about Aunty Ratbag or school or his parents, but the gravedigger could guess. He knew that Danny must be desperate and no one should blame a desperate child for making a wrong decision.

The kettle whistled and the gravedigger's mind wandered further. Twenty years further to the grim Greezy morning when the gravedigger had met another lonely boy, a boy who looked a lot like Danny. The gravedigger had seen a strength and courage in the boy's thin body that would have been extraordinary in a grown man. In a young child it was unbelievable.

Lionel Gruntfuttock had smashed a window and climbed into the gravedigger's hut to steal food. The gravedigger had caught him red-handed, but he was not angry because the gravedigger understood hunger. So he bandaged Lionel's cut hands and cooked him breakfast. And when the boy was drinking a second mug of the best hot chocolate he had ever tasted, the gravedigger gave Lionel Gruntfuttock his first lesson in professional crime.

Windows were for amateurs, the gravedigger had explained. Professionals use the front door. They pick the lock, take what they want, leave no evidence and vanish into the night.

In the months that followed the gravedigger had taught

Lionel the art of house breaking: the digging of tunnels; how to scale walls and disable alarms; how to slip a night latch with a credit card and open a deadlock with a bent pin; and which are the best explosives for every burgling situation.

'And how much to use, because there's no point blowing a safe if you destroy what's inside,' the gravedigger had explained, patiently.

Danny's father was an eager student.

The gravedigger did not mean to turn him into a crook. It's just a bit of fun, he had told himself. And the boy knows it's only a game.

It was an error of judgement the gravedigger had regretted ever since. And now he had steered Danny on to the same path. Not deliberately. He had not known King Bone's plan. But the consequences were the same.

'It's about time you took your own advice and stopped meddling,' he told himself. 'And let every fox take care of its own tail.'

The gravedigger took his tea outside to finish.

And saw Danny crouching behind Mr Phlegm's car.

And saw Aunty Ratbag turn the corner from Slugg's.

The gravedigger was about to shout a warning, when he remembered his promise. He had interfered enough and it had always gone wrong. So he poured the dregs of his tea on the ground and went back to his hole.

Chapter 24

THE SMOKING GUN, PART TWO

AUNTY RATBAG STOMPED across the empty school playground and barged into headmistress' office. Her six desperate dogs did not wait to be told. They knew what their mistress expected, and they squatted on the carpet and peed.

The headmistress and Mr Phlegm gulped and quaked.

'How dare you punish Danny without my permission!' snarled Aunty Ratbag. 'If it happens again I'll reach down your throats, rip your kidneys out and feed them to my dogs! Have I made myself clear?'

The two un-educators nodded. Trickles of wee ran down their legs and mingled with the pools of dog piddle spreading across the carpet.

'I'll fetch the brat home with me now. Where is he?'

'Errrm...?' m-m-m-mumbled Mr Phlegm. 'He d-d-d-didn't...'

'Didn't what?' Suddenly, it was Aunty Ratbag's turn to gulp and quake.

'...c-c-c-come to sc-sc-sc-school this m-m-m-morning.'

Aunty Ratbag almost fainted. Danny had run away and she had only had him a few days!

Aunty Ratbag raced from the school and fled, unthinking, across the graveyard. She reached her house and searched her shed. There was no trace of Danny.

Maybe he's hiding in his bedroom, she thought as she turned the handle of the kitchen door.

Aunty Ratbag was inside before she realised what it meant. The door was unlocked.

She had been robbed!

Chapter 25

THE IRON KEY

'SO YOU REALLY are a thief,' observed the new girl coolly. 'A bad one too.'

Danny's cheeks flushed.

'I saw you following me,' said the new girl. 'So I set a trap and you walked right in. Is that how your parents were caught? The newspapers didn't say how the police tracked them down.'

Danny turned to face the new girl. The mound of clothes and broken toys and ripped books was between them. Danny was too embarrassed and confused to speak. He could feel bits of toy stuffing caught in his hair and tickling his face.

'What are you looking for?' she asked in a tone of voice that said she did not really care. 'Money? My iPad?'

Danny shook his head. 'A key,' he mumbled. 'You found an old iron key in a rabbit hole. I need it.'

The new girl blinked in surprise. 'How do you know about my key?'

Danny shook his head. How could he tell her about King Bones and the quest? The new girl would never believe him. It was too ridiculous.

'If you don't tell me I'll call the police,' said the new girl, taking her mobile phone from her pocket. She started to dial the number.

'Not the police!' begged Danny.

The new girl crossed her arms and waited, whilst Danny took a deep breath and began to talk.

When he finished the new girl reached straight for her phone. It was the most ridiculous story that she had ever heard.

'I'm not lying,' gasped Danny. 'And I can prove it!'

Danny showed the new girl King Bones' little finger.

'It's a skeleton key,' he explained. 'It can open any lock in the world. It's how I got into your house.'

The new girl's index finger stopped half of a millimetre above the last 9 of 999.

'How does it work?' she asked.

'I don't know, exactly,' Danny admitted. 'The king said it uses pagan magic. If there's a locked room I can show you.'

The new girl led Danny through the house to her step stepfather's study. If Danny was lying – and she was nearly certain that he was lying – she would call the police to arrest him and if he tried to run away she would set the dog on him.

The new girl rattled the study door. It was locked. It always was. Her step stepfather had the only key. The new girl stepped aside to give Danny space to make a fool of himself.

Danny put the skeleton key close to the lock and held his breath and waited for the miracle to happen.

It did not.

The new girl rolled her eyes. When would Danny stop pretending and admit his story was a pack of stupid lies? He was the worst liar she had ever known. He was worse at fibbing than he was at stealing. She began to dial the number for the police.

The phone fell from the new girl's hand. Before her disbelieving eyes, the whitish-grey bones glowed blue and changed shape and became a key. The new girl gaped as Danny pushed the skeleton key into the lock.

Click!

Danny turned the handle and pushed the door.

The new girl's step stepfather's study really was a museum. A private museum filled with priceless objects, and many rare and ancient books.

In a glass display case rested the golden shield of Alexander the Great, the most famous general who has ever lived. Next to it was the sword of Damocles and the feather underpants of Montezuma, the last king of the Aztecs. In another case was the toga worn by Julius Caesar on the Ides of March. It was stained with Caesar's blood and punctured with 22 holes ripped by his assassins' daggers.

Beside the toga, in a crystal casket, lay the strangest treasure in the collection. It was a set of false teeth that had once belonged to Timur the Lame, the cruellest man in human history. His enemies called him '*the Lame*' because he walked with a limp.

Timur was a descendent of the terrible Genghis Khan, a monster who killed more people than the Black Death. Timur wanted to beat Genghis' record for murder, so he invaded Asia and chopped the heads from ten million women and children. He used their skulls to build a pyramid. Even Genghis was not that cruel.

Timur's dentures were made with real teeth pulled from the gums of an Indian princess. Timur was jealous of the princess' perfect smile. His own teeth were brown and rotten from drinking sherbet, so he wore the princess' instead. The teeth were set in green jade, carved to fit over Timur's gums. The jade was a mistake. The green colour gave Timur the smile of a rotting corpse, although no one dared to tell him.

Danny went from one exhibit to the next too amazed to speak.

'My step stepfather found them,' said the new girl. There was a hint of pride in her voice. Although they despised each other, her step stepfather was the closest thing the new girl had to a parent. 'He's a famous archaeologist. You've probably seen him on TV.'

Danny was not interested in the man's profession. He was too busy trying to work out how anyone could have a step stepfather.

'My mother died when I was young,' explained the new girl in a matter-of-fact way. It was a tragic tale and the new girl could only tell it without tears because she had rehearsed it many times in the hope that, one day, someone would ask.

Except no one in Greezy cared, so Danny was the first person to hear her performance.

'She was hit by a bus,' said the new girl, without emotion.

Her dog moaned. The new girl had trained it to act sad in the right places.

'A red London double-decker bus, the number 13 from Trafalgar Square to Golders Green. It was the last of the old-fashioned Routemaster buses still working. It happened on Regent Street. Mum was taking me to Hamley's toyshop to buy me a present for my birthday. She crossed the road without looking and...'

The dog grovelled on its belly and covered its eyes with its huge paws.

'Then dad married my stepmother. They had only been married twenty minutes when he was hit by a double-decker too. He'd hired the bus to take the wedding guests from the church to the reception. It reversed over him in the church car park,' the new girl explained. 'Dad didn't want to be reminded of mum, so he had rented a green bus instead of a red one. The car park was surrounded by trees, so it was sort of camouflaged and he didn't see it coming.'

'Then stepmother remarried. Stepfather was a kind man. I think we would have been a happy family. But we never had a chance because he was run over too.'

'A bus?' asked Danny.

The new girl nodded. 'Then stepmother married my step stepfather. He hates me.'

At the mention of the new girl's step stepfather the dog growled.

'What about your step mum?' asked Danny.

'She loved me, but she was killed in another road accident.'

'Another bus?'

The new girl shook her head. 'A taxi. After mum and dad and stepfather, my stepmother avoided public transport. Then my step stepfather married my step stepmother.'

The dog growled even louder when it heard the words 'step stepmother'.

'She's worse than he is.'

'Then we have something in common,' said Danny brightly. 'I live with my aunt. She hates me too.'

Danny beamed at the new girl and, a moment later, her

mask broke and the new girl smiled back. Somehow she looked exactly the same and completely different.

'I'm Audrey,' said the new girl and they shook hands. 'Sorry about my note.'

Danny remembered Audrey's bedroom and blushed. 'And I'm sorry about breaking all your stuff,' he mumbled.

The new girl laughed. 'Really, don't mention it. I couldn't care less about any of that stuff. They're just gifts from my Godparents. They promised Mum and Dad to look after me if I ever needed help. Buying me expensive presents stops them feeling guilty for breaking their word and leaving me with my step stepparents. Shall we look for the key?'

As they searched the new girl told Danny how the key had ended up in her step stepfather's collection. 'It was my own fault. I was excited to find something old and, because he's an archaeologist, I showed it to him. He snatched it from my hand and gave me a twenty-pound note. When I asked for it back, he said it was far too valuable for a child and, anyway, it his now because he had paid me for it.'

They found the key wrapped in a black satin handkerchief. Danny unfolded the silk and gasped. He was expecting a piece of rough wrought iron, but the key was beautiful. It was a work of art created by the finest craftsman of Anglo Saxon Greezy. The metal was smooth as glass and the black surfaces were covered in intricate golden drawings of dragons and sea serpents.

Audrey put the key in her pocket. The weight felt good.

The two children left the study together. Danny was about to re-lock the door with the skeleton key, when Audrey stopped him. She took the twenty-pound note from her purse,

wrapped the money in the black satin and put the handkerchief on the shelf.

'Now it belongs to me again,' she whispered.

Chapter 26

THE SECRET CHAMBER UNDER THE CHURCH NEXT TO THE DOG FOOD FACTORY (NOT THE ONE OPPOSITE THE CAT FOOD FACTORY)

THE CHURCH SMELT of dust and candle wax, and so did the cross-eyed vicar who glared at the children as suspiciously as any shopkeeper. The vicar did not like children. He had good reason. Beulah's gang had smashed his stained glass windows, stolen the poor box and set fire to the pews.

The vicar was about to tell them to clear off, when he recognised Audrey. She was the foreign child whose step stepfather had donated a thousand pounds to repair the damage. In return for his money, the archaeologist asked for a few hours to examine the church in peace. So when Audrey told him they had come to light a candle for her dead parents and stepparents the vicar pretended to believe her.

'Take your time,' said the vicar. 'I would stay with you,' he added, examining his fingernails and pulling an earlobe. 'But I have an important meeting with, errrm…? The Bishop? About an, errrm…? A new roof for the church?'

The vicar's real meeting was with a plate of Beef Twisters and a bottle of beer.

Audrey was glad to see the back of the vicar's bald head.

'He's a horrible man,' she whispered to Danny. 'He gives me the creeps.'

'Me too,' agreed Danny. He liked agreeing with Audrey.

The heallwahrift was in a side chapel of the timeworn church. It was so large it was hard to see the whole thing. Danny and Audrey stepped back to get a better look. For a few seconds the sun broke through the clouds. Light filled the church and the heallwahrift blazed with colour.

Danny recognised King Bones by his armour and golden crown and his purple cloak. He was riding a magnificent white stallion into a fast-flowing river followed by his brave warriors. The king was more than a bit fat. He was obese. His armour was stretched tight over his bulging belly and his fat bum sagged down both sides of the saddle. He looked a lot like Mr Phlegm, only taller, fatter, fitter, braver and slightly less cross-eyed.

The queen and her ladies-in-waiting and the wives of the warriors were beautiful. Their hair was the colour of buttercups and their eyes were cornflower blue. The queen was standing on the riverbank, weeping and waving a silk handkerchief. The colour of the handkerchief matched her eyes.

Only the queen was shown crying. Her ladies-in-waiting and the other wives were rolling their eyes and shouting at their stupid husbands.

Danny looked around to be sure they were alone.

'Come on,' he whispered and they crept behind the heallwahrift.

It was dark and musty, and spiders scurried over their faces. They had to feel their way along the wall with their fingertips, until they found the faint outline of a door and a deep keyhole. The iron key was a perfect fit. Audrey turned it and they heard a heavy *'clunk!'*. They pushed the door and it swung inwards with a creak.

They were at the top of a steep spiral staircase that led down deep under the church. Flaming torches, fixed to the damp walls with rusting brackets, lit the way.

'Hello!' called Danny. 'Is anyone there?'

His voice echoed down the stairs.

'Hello! Hello! Hello! Is anyone there? Is anyone there? Is anyone there?'

Silence answered with a puff of stale wind that flickered the flaming torches.

Holding hands, the children took the first step together.

The staircase corkscrewed clockwise. Danny counted the steps. Ten, twenty, thirty. The staircase went on and on. Forty, fifty. They were deep underground. Danny could feel the colossal weight of the earth above pressing down upon their heads.

Sixty, seventy. Danny stopped counting. There were exactly seventy steps.

The entrance to the secret chamber was through an arch carved into the living rock. The floor was hidden by swirling mist. The children stepped into the mist and ghostly tentacles of white wrapped around their legs and twisted up their bodies.

King Bones' tomb was a warm and friendly place filled with laughter, but the queen's tomb was sad and chill. The flaming torches gave light, but no heat, and the light was thin and pale. There was no throne or piles of treasure. The room was stripped bare.

So were the skeletons lined up to greet the children. Bare, naked bones, without a stitch of clothing or a copper ring.

The queen was naked too.

And, most terrible of all, she was headless.

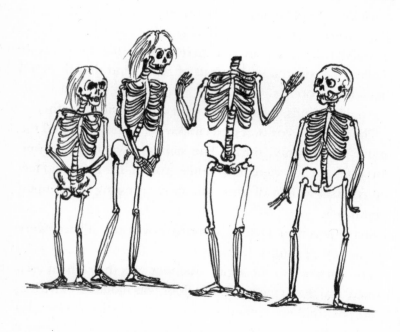

Chapter 27

THE HEADLESS QUEEN

THE WIVES AND ladies-in-waiting were sobbing and pulling at the remnants of their buttercup hair.

'A cruel man did it!' they wailed. 'He came during daylight when we sleep and took everything! Our clothes! Our jewellery! Everything! And he snapped the queen's neck and stole her head!'

'And I gave him the key!' whispered Audrey.

'He took it from you,' Danny reminded her. 'But how did he know about the secret chamber?'

'It's what he does,' said Audrey. 'Step stepfather travels around the world finding ancient treasures and selling them to museums. He must have read about the secret chamber in one of his old books. I wondered why we moved to Greezy. He's got an exhibition opening tomorrow at the British Museum in London.'

'But our clothes and treasures belong to us!' wailed the women. 'No one has the right to take them, even if we are dead. All these centuries we have waited to be rescued and now, when the door is finally open, we cannot leave! How can we go before the king naked and the queen without her head?'

The queen put her hands to her mouth that was not there. Danny heard the scream that did not come.

'There's only one thing to do,' said Danny firmly. 'Audrey and I will go to London and steal it back.'

'Would you really?' said the women. 'Will you do that for us?'

They clustered around the children stroking their hair and faces. Danny and Audrey cringed at the touch of their bare bones and the creaking of dry ribs as the skeletons hugged them.

The headless queen walked towards them. Even naked and without a skull there was no mistaking her majesty.

The children knelt before her and the queen stretched out a bare arm. In the tips of her fingers she held a blue silk handkerchief. It was the same handkerchief shown in the heallwahrift.

Danny had seen enough films to understand. The queen was appointing Danny as her champion to fight for her honour.

Danny reached out to take the handkerchief. Becoming the queen's champion would make up for the name-calling and Aunty Ratbag and the cold broccoli soup and the dog eggs and everything else he had suffered. It was the start of a better life!

Until the queen gave the handkerchief to Audrey.

Chapter 28

THE WRATH OF KINGS

THE CHURCH CLOCK was striking six o'clock when they reached the graveyard.

'Hold my hand,' said Danny. 'And don't be scared when it gets weird.'

Audrey pulled a face. She had never been scared of anything and she certainly did not need to hold Danny's hand...

...until the graveyard began to grow and the twinkling lights of Aunty Ratbag's house raced away into the night. Trees erupted from the earth, and Audrey grabbed Danny's hand and squeezed it hard.

'The fog comes next,' he warned.

The first wisps of mist curled though the air and thickened into fog. A sea of white fog rolled in from every side, submerging the children.

'What's that noise?' whimpered Audrey. She had never been so frightened.

Danny thought it was better not to say. Through the fog pairs of pale blue lights emerged. Audrey gulped when she saw their swords and armour and their iron helmets and their skeleton faces.

'Take me to the king,' demanded Danny and the skeletons obeyed.

The skeletons led the children to the stone door and beat their bony fists on the hard rock.

'Who disturbs the king's peace?' called the king's steward.

'Danny Bouygues,' croaked Danny, the words stuck in his throat. He was afraid too.

'And Audrey De La Tour,' said Audrey, proud and clear. 'It's a French name,' she whispered to Danny. 'My father – my real father - was French.'

The stone door swung open.

*****

Danny had never seen such rage. As the children told their tale the king and his warriors gripped their weapons until their knuckles cracked.

The children finished and waited for the king to speak. The huscarls and warriors kept their silence. What would the king do? He had been buried these fourteen centuries. Had he lost his courage?

Slowly King Bones rose from his golden throne. He looked about at his warriors, and then he threw back his purple cloak and drew his broadsword and held the mighty blade aloft.

'We ride for London!' he roared.

His warriors took up the cry. 'To London!' they cheered, loud enough to wake the dead.

The warriors' horses had been buried with them. The horses took up too much space, so the warriors had taken them to pieces and stored the bones in barrels.

'You'll need food,' said the king, as his warriors got to work reassembling the horses. 'It's a long way to London.' The king was shouting to be heard above the Anglo Saxon cursing of his men. Many years had passed since the warriors had taken the horses apart and they had forgotten how to put the bones back together.

Ignoring the foul language of his soldiers, King Bones continued: 'My warriors can ride to Hell and back, but children must eat. You have until seven o'clock. It will take until then to resurrect our mounts. Don't keep us waiting.'

The children bowed and ran from the tomb.

Chapter 29

COME OUT TO PLAY?

THE CHILDREN HAD no choice where to go for food. Audrey's house was too far away to get there and back by 7 o'clock. Danny's pride stopped him suggesting the gravedigger. So it had to be Aunty Ratbag's.

'If only I hadn't given the twenty pounds back,' moaned Audrey. 'Then we could have bought something from a corner shop. There's one nearby. Maybe we could steal something?'

'Shush!' shushed Danny. He did not want to think about shoplifting, especially from *that* corner shop. Anyway, they had reached Aunty Ratbag's house. Danny knew his Aunt was home; he could hear the television in the front room.

The skeleton key remembered the shape that opened the kitchen door. A bowl of broccoli soup was on the table. Light and noise from the television slipped under the cracks at the bottom of the doors between the kitchen and the front room. Danny held King Bones' finger to his lips telling Audrey to keep quiet.

On tiptoe Danny walked to the fridge. He found some cheese and a packet of ham. He was about to take them, when he stopped, remembering the gravedigger's warning and the countless reflections of the shopkeeper's face and Audrey's broken room. Danny realised that he was not standing at the top of a slippery slope. He was already sliding down.

Danny closed the fridge door. He preferred to go hungry. But it was too late.

Click!

The kitchen light switched on, blinding the children with its bright whiteness. Aunty Ratbag crossed the kitchen in three long strides, slammed the door and locked it with heavy bolts. She had been waiting for Danny to return, counting and recounting every biscuit and slice of bread until she knew exactly what and how much Danny had taken.

'No one steals from me,' she hissed.

Her face was twisted into a wicked snarl. Seeing Audrey, Aunty Ratbag grabbed the girl's arm and lifted her clean off the ground. 'And who's this brat? Your partner in crime?'

'I can explain,' stammered Danny.

Aunty Ratbag dropped Audrey. The girl fell in a crumpled heap.

'No explanation's needed. Thieving's in your blood. It's in your bones. I've spoken to your teacher. The fat fool says you have been bunking off school. Two days you lasted. Two days! Even your useless father did better than that. I blame that filthy woman you call a mother. The dirty French...!'

Aunty Ratbag did not finish her sentence.

Danny flung himself at Aunty Ratbag. No one called his mother names and got away with it.

It was no use. Danny's valour was in vain. Aunty Ratbag was too strong and quick. She caught him midair and flung him to the ground. The skeleton key slipped from Danny's hand, skidded across the kitchen floor and disappeared under the fridge.

Aunty Ratbag grabbed the children by their hair and carried

them upstairs to Danny's bedroom, ignoring their struggles and squeals of pain. With a cackle of demonic fury, she drove the bolts home, trapping the children inside.

Danny beat on the door and kicked, pointlessly. The door was made from solid oak and his strongest kick left no dent. Defeated, Danny sat on the bed and wept. Their adventure was over. He had failed.

Audrey was looking out of the barred window, hoping to see King Bones and signal to him. But the fog was too thick. She sat on the bed beside Danny and put an arm around his shoulders.

'It's OK,' she whispered, knowing it was not.

'Everything will be fine,' she said, knowing that nothing would be fine ever again for her or Danny. Audrey had missed her chance to escape from her wretched existence in Greezy. King Bones would leave without them and ride to London. He would think they had turned coward and he would never forgive them.

Downstairs, they heard Aunty Ratbag telephoning the police.

'I won't have the thieving swine in my house for another night,' she screamed. 'He takes money from my purse. He's stolen my silver spoons. He bites my dogs, he wets his bed and he poos in his room. Take him away and throw him in prison with his wretched parents. It's what he deserves!'

Danny's face broke. 'I don't wet the bed. And I didn't rob her purse or steal anything, except a ham sandwich. And some biscuits and a chocolate. But I've never hurt her rotten dogs and I've never pooed in my room. Honest I didn't.'

'I know,' said Audrey and she stroked Danny's head. She

never thought he did. Not even when she saw the poo in the corner by the window. Audrey had scooped enough to recognise a dog egg.

Danny wiped his eyes and sat up straight. Audrey believing him was enough to make him feel better.

They sat side-by-side on Danny's blanket, waiting. 'What will happen now, do you think?' asked Audrey.

'The lady in the green coat will take me away again, I suppose.' said Danny. 'And Aunty Ratbag will call your step stepparents and…'

The church clock struck 7.

*****

Aunty Ratbag had finished ranting on the phone to the police and she returned to her television programme. She was watching the news about a terrible famine in Africa.

'Serves you right!' she hooted with delight at the pictures of starving children with swollen tummies. 'There are too many brats in the world. We could do with a few less mouths to feed.' She took a big bite of chocolate cake for her worms to eat.

Ding-dong!

The doorbell rang, setting her ugly dogs yapping and running in circles, chasing their fluffy tail.

'Shut up!' screamed Aunty Ratbag and she kicked the dogs and slapped them with her sharp hands. The dogs whimpered and cowered.

The police had arrived more quickly than Aunty Ratbag expected and now they were here she was regretting calling them. She did not want to loose Danny. She was having too much fun with him. Then she saw the silver lining.

I'll let the police arrest the brat and keep in the cells overnight, she told herself. And tomorrow morning I'll be '*nice*' and rescue him!

The doorbell rang again.

'Stop ringing the damn bell! You'll wear the battery out!'

Aunty Ratbag peered through the glass panel in the front door. She could not see anyone in the thick fog.

'Who is it?' she called. 'What do you want?'

A dark figure appeared.

'Is Danny in?' The voice was muffled. 'Can he come out to play?'

In all her seventy years, Aunty Ratbag had never been so furious. How dare Danny's horrible friends disturb her evening's entertainment!

'Come out to play!' she roared and she wrenched the door almost off its hinges. 'I'll give you come out to play!'

The words froze on her lips.

Aunty Ratbag was expecting a child, not a full-grown man. Especially a tall man wearing a purple cloak with the hood pulled over his face.

King Bones threw back the hood. His crown glittered. His eyes glowed hot red.

Aunty Ratbag fainted. She was never the same woman again.

King Bones stepped over the fallen woman and ran upstairs to Danny's bedroom. 'Stand back,' he ordered, as he drew his broadsword. With a single blow, he smashed the door to splinters. 'Come with me. The army is ready. There's not a moment to lose.'

The children chased King Bones down the stairs and stepped over Aunty Ratbag. The old lady was sitting on the floor, leaning against the wall. Her hair had turned pure white and she was mumbling to herself.

'Come out to play?' Aunty Ratbag's voice was weak and confused. 'Come out to play?'

A gust of wind opened a window in the fog revealing the skeleton army, mounted and ready. Spears and armour sparkled in the moonlight. Skeleton horses pawed the ground with their hooves. After their long confinement they were impatient to begin.

After 1,400 years, King Bones and his army were riding to war.

Chapter 30

THE BRITISH MUSEUM

IT WAS THE foggiest night in history.

On such a night people see – or think they see – the strangest things. A farmer in Scotland claimed the Loch Ness Monster crawled from the water and chased his sheep. Students in Wales said a spaceship landed in a cornfield and aliens tried to abduct them. And motorists trapped in fog-bound traffic on the M1 motorway swore they saw a horde of skeleton warriors riding skeleton horses leap the central reservation and charge in the direction of London.

Danny and Audrey were seated behind the king, wrapped in his purple cloak to keep them warm.

'We can't stay on the road,' shouted Audrey, above the pounding crack of iron-shod hooves striking tarmac. 'We'll cause an accident.'

'We can follow the railway lines,' said Danny. 'They'll take us into the centre of London.'

The fog had closed Euston Station or more people would have seen the column of mounted warriors jump the ticket barrier and gallop across the station concourse.

A policeman stopped the traffic on the Euston Road to let the horses and their riders cross safely into Upper Woburn Place, the road that led to the British Museum.

'It's the Queen's Household Calvary wearing fancy dress,'

explained the policeman to some frightened American tourists. The policeman was wearing a uniform so the tourists chose to believe him instead of trusting their own eyes and common sense. The tourists shivered in their tartan shorts and anoraks and asked the policeman to take their photograph as the skeleton army cantered past.

The skeleton army arrived in Russell Square. There was a large garden in the middle of the Square surrounded by a fence of high iron railings topped with spikes. The garden was closed for the night and, apart from a sleeping tramp, no one saw the skeleton horses leap the railings.

'The back door to the British Museum is over there,' said Audrey, pointing through the swirling murk towards a tall building swathed in fog. 'You'll have to leave your horses here. There's no room for them inside the Museum. Don't worry. They'll be safe. The gates are padlocked at night, so they can't wander off and no one will find them.'

The warriors dismounted and tied their steeds to the metal railings. At once, the horses lowered their heads to graze on the succulent grass and flowers. It was their first meal in more than a thousand years.

Audrey had taken charge because she had been to the British Museum once before. Also it was her step stepfather's exhibition and she had always dreamed of being the hero in a real adventure.

With his bare hands, King Bones pulled apart two iron railings to make a man-sized exit from the garden. The iron railings were solid metal, two-metres high and thick as the handle of a tennis racket. King Bones bent them as if they were made of rubber.

Audrey was the first through the gap, with Danny and King Bones close on her heels. Behind them, in single file, a column of huscarls and ordinary warriors followed, with their weapons drawn and ready for combat.

Audrey knocked on the back door of the Museum and pretended she was a frightened little girl, who had lost her parents in the fog and did not know where to go. To make her act extra convincing, Audrey burst into snivelling sobs. When the security guards opened the back door to help the little girl, strong warriors barged in, overpowered the security guards and quickly tied them up and stuffed rags into their mouths.

'It's this way,' said Audrey wiping the crocodile tears from her eyes and enjoying the hateful glares of the security guards. 'The Special Exhibition is in a room off the Great Court. And the Great Court is right in the centre of the Museum.'

Audrey led the way, with Danny one step behind. The children were in the next room before they realised they were on their own. They hurried back and found the skeletons gathered around a sign fixed to the wall. The warriors were muttering to each other in worried whispers.

Danny pushed his way to the front. 'What's the matter?'

'Dogs,' whispered King Bones loudly. 'The sign says there are guard dogs in the museum. My warriors will fight man or beast, but not dogs.'

'You've got to be joking!' hissed Audrey. 'You're scared of dogs!'

'You weren't afraid of Aunty Ratbag's dogs,' said Danny, reminding the king.

'Were those dogs?' said King Bones. 'I thought they were diseased rats!'

Danny remembered his visits to the graveyard and how scared he had been. 'You have to face your fears,' he told King Bones. 'If you give in, they'll get bigger and bigger until you're scared of everything. Faint heart never won fair maid!'

King Bones was not sure that he agreed with Mr Bouygues' little saying.

'I'm already married,' the king reminded Danny. 'So I don't want to win a maid, even if she's the fairest girl in England. And the queen would be furious if she thought I had come down to London to find myself a girlfriend. Perhaps you and Audrey should go on alone and we'll keep watch here?'

The loyal huscarls nodded their skulls vigorously, agreeing with their king's wise words and making their iron helmets rattle like cow bells.

'You have to come,' pleaded Danny. 'Audrey and I aren't strong enough to carry everything.'

But it was no use. King Bones would not be moved. He had made his final decision and he would never change his mind, no matter what.

'Then you'll have to go back to Greezy empty handed,' said Audrey. 'And tell the queen that you were too frightened to rescue her head, and get her clothes and jewellery back. I expect she'll be even more furious when she hears that.'

The king was scared of dogs, but he was terrified of his wife.

'Death or glory,' croaked the king to encourage his warriors. He did not sound very convincing.

'Death or glory,' mumbled his warriors in answer. They did not sound very convinced.

'Oh shut up,' shushed Audrey. 'You're already dead, or have you forgotten? Now keep up or you'll get lost. The

British Museum's a maze of interconnecting rooms and levels and basements and dead ends and staircases that lead to nowhere. You're lucky I know my way around.'

'Maybe we should take a map?' said Danny, spotting a pile of tourist maps on a shelf beside the tied up security guards. The maps had been left for visitors to help themselves. The maps showed every room of the museum and how to navigate between them easily.

'We don't need a map,' whispered Audrey. 'I could find my way around with my eyes closed.'

Just in case, Danny put a map in his jacket pocket.

'And try to be quiet,' Audrey hissed. 'A herd of wild elephants would make less noise than you lot.'

Being the hero was going to Audrey's head.

You're beginning to sound a lot like Aunty Ratbag, thought Danny.

Audrey took them into the next room and up a grand spiralling marble staircase, passed walls decorated with mosaics taken from Roman palaces and villas. The skeletons did their best to be quiet, but it was impossible. Their bone feet clattered and skidded on the marble steps, and they barged into each other. Their shields banged and their weapons clashed.

'Honestly!' moaned Audrey.

At the top of the stairs they entered a line of rooms connected by tall double doors.

'This way!' hissed Audrey confidently. 'We're almost there!'

This was the first time Danny had visited the British Museum. But in the same way that a young eel instinctively knows the right way from the Sargasso Sea where it was born, to the distant river where its parents had lived many years before, somehow Danny knew that Audrey had taken a wrong turn.

He opened the map, quietly so Audrey would not hear. Danny was good with maps. Mr Bouygues had taught him how to use a compass and read Ordinance Survey maps before Danny could walk properly. And when he was five, Mr Bouygues took Danny to a remote valley in Dartmoor. He gave Danny a compass and a map, and left the boy to find his own way back to the car. Mr Bouygues kept watch from a distance, but Danny did not know that.

The museum map was colour-coded and easy to read. Even Mr Phlegm could have managed to find his way around without getting lost. Danny quickly located the back door to the museum where they had started. From there, the Great Court was straight ahead and on the same level. But Audrey had turned left, gone up the marble staircase and turned left again.

Danny studied the glass display cases and saw they were filled with long wooden boxes. Danny had a closer look. The boxes were covered in strange writing. Hieroglyphs! The boxes were the sarcophagi the Ancient Egyptians used as coffins to bury their mummies. Danny checked the map. As he thought, they were in the Exhibition of Egyptian Antiquities.

'Audrey,' he whispered, touching her lightly on the shoulder to get her attention. 'I think you've made a mistake.'

Audrey snatched the map from Danny's hands and held it upside down.

'The other way up,' suggested Danny.

'What?'

'You've got the map upside down.'

'There's no up or down,' snapped Audrey. 'It's a map! You can read it anyway you like!'

Danny fell silent. This was the same Audrey who had written the six-word note on his first day at school.

Audrey studied the map and the warriors pressed into the room behind her. Their bones and weapons tap-tapped on the glass display cases. Audrey put a finger on a part of the map that was coloured yellow.

'We're here,' she whispered.

She was pointing at the ladies toilet in the basement cafeteria on the other side of the building.

Danny shook his head and pointed to the place on the map where they were actually standing.

'That's where I meant,' hissed Audrey. She sounded angry, but her confidence was draining away. Being the hero was harder than she had thought. Audrey's head was spinning. In the dark the British Museum was so different. She was lost.

'We'll have to go back,' she whispered. 'To where we came in and start again.'

King Bones shook his skull. In the confined space of the museum it was impossible to turn the army around. They had to go forwards.

Danny took the map from Audrey's hands. She did not resist. Danny traced a winding route from the Exhibition of Egyptian Antiquities through the British Museum's many chambers and staircases to the Great Court. It was a long way round, but it would have to do. Danny felt a rush of pride that he had solved the puzzle, not Audrey. It was his adventure again and he would take them to the finish line.

Then Danny remembered that Audrey was his friend – his *only* friend.

Danny screwed the map into a ball and threw it away.

'It's a rubbish map,' he lied. 'I don't know where we are. When you came before you must have been in this room. Where did you go afterwards?'

Audrey tried to think. Danny was relying on her. The skeleton army needed her and she was Queen Bones' champion too.

Danny crossed his fingers. If Audrey did not remember soon he would have to take control.

Audrey forced her mind back to the day she had spent in the British Museum. Her step stepfather took ages looking at the exhibits of dead Egyptians and the trinkets they were buried with. Afterwards, he took Audrey to the restaurant in the Great Court. Suddenly, Audrey remembered every twist and turn.

'This way,' she said. She sounded confident again, but her voice had lost its arrogance.

Audrey led them past the Egyptian mummies, swathed in bandages and across a narrow glass bridge they approached a round building in a huge open space with a glass roof above their heads. The skeletons stood in awed amazement. It was the Great Court of the British Museum.

'Well done, Audrey!' whispered Danny. 'No one else could have done it.'

Audrey blushed at the compliment. If only Danny knew how close I had come to failing, she thought.

From the glass bridge there was a staircase that led down to the ground level. The staircase spiraled about the round building that stood in the centre of the Great Court. Danny counted the steps. There were exactly seventy.

When they reached the bottom of the staircase, the skeletons spread out and stood in awed amazement, gazing upwards at the wondrous curving glass roof.

It was the biggest room they had ever seen. It dwarfed King Bones' tomb and the Great Hall of Greezy Castle. And Greezy Castle had been the largest building in England.

As they stood gawping, something sharp nudged Audrey's head. It was King Bones' stallion. The horse did not want to be left behind and it had decided to follow. Without its covering of muscle, the horse was small enough to step through the gap King Bones had made in the railings.

'Shoo!' hissed Audrey.

The horse did not move.

'He'll have to come with us,' whispered Danny. 'If you send him away, he will only get lost and he can't make more noise than the other skeletons.'

Reluctantly, Audrey agreed.

Chapter 31

THE SPECIAL EXHIBITION OF ANGLO SAXON TREASURES

As Audrey had predicted, her step stepfather's Special Exhibition of Anglo Saxon Treasures was in a room off the Great Court.

The huscarls formed a fighting column, four abreast, and forced their way past the ticket barrier. The warriors of the fryd came behind in an unruly mob.

They entered the exhibition and staggered to a halt.

The dresses and jewellery of the ladies-in-waiting were displayed on life-sized models behind thick bulletproof glass. They were more magnificent than Danny or Audrey could ever have imagined.

The dresses were made from fine woollen cloth, dyed in multi-coloured hues - blue, yellow, green and violet - and embroidered with silver thread and freckled with pearls. The queen and her ladies-in-waiting had spun the cloth and made the dresses themselves. Their brooches, rings and necklaces were cast in purest gold, decorated with intricate designs of garnets and rare lapis lazuli from distant Afghanistan.

The clothes of the ordinary women were simpler. But although their jewellery was only bronze or polish horn, it was more precious than gold to its owners.

The warriors rushed around the exhibition searching for

their wives' belongings. From every side the children heard cries as warriors recognized things they had known.

'I remember the first time she wore that dress!' gasped one skeleton.

'I gave her that ring on our wedding day!' said another.

'That belt belonged to my great great grandmother!' whispered a third. 'It's the prized heirloom of my family, passed down for six generations. Great great granny Helga brought it across the North Sea from the forests of Germany.'

King Bones strode onwards, with the children at his side. In the middle of the exhibition they found the queen's skull. It was locked in a glass box bolted to the ground. The queen's head was still and lifeless. Her crown shone dismally. The sight of it filled the children with sadness. They turned away, unable to look.

King Bones stood before his wife's bleached dead skull and remembered how beautiful she had been in life. Where the children saw bone and sparse strands of brittle yellow hair, the king saw the fresh living face of the women he had loved and missed for so many centuries.

The king grasped the glass box in his strong hands and heaved. But the box was fixed too firmly to the ground. So the king drew his broadsword. The sword sang as it flew from the scabbard and, with a single mighty swing, the king sliced the top from the box as if it was a boiled egg.

The noise was instant and deafening. Bells and sirens screamed. Lights flashed.

'The box was alarmed!' shouted Danny. 'Quick! Take everything! The police will be here in minutes!'

The warriors smashed the glass display cases and took the

things that belong to their loved ones. More alarms rang out.
The skeletons rolled the treasure in their wives' dresses and
stuffed the rolls beneath their armour inside their empty
chests.

'Hurry!' begged Audrey.

But the king would not be hurried. Kings Bones lifted the
queen's skull and brought it to his lip-less lips and kissed it.

'My love,' he whispered. 'What have they done to you?'

'Come on!' shouted Audrey and the two children pushed

and pulled the king. It was no use. The king's legs were fixed to the ground as firmly as the box had been. King Bones was lost in the memories of long ago.

The barking of dogs broke the spell.

Chapter 32

DEATH OR GLORY

FROM EVERY CORNER of London, police cars sped towards the British Museum. The first to arrive sealed the exits and waited for Scotland Yard's elite armed police units to arrive. These were the same police officers that had arrested Mr and Mrs Bouygues. They wore black helmets and black armour. Some carried black shields. Their faces were hidden behind black masks. And each had a black machine gun with a black torch strapped to the barrel.

The Museum security guards were waiting to show the police in. They had seen the skeleton warriors, with their swords and spears, on the CCTV. The security guards were not paid to battle the undead and they had decided to leave the fighting to the professionals.

'Stand back,' said the policeman in charge, who was actually a policewoman. Her name was Inspector Sands. 'This is a job for the professionals,' and she led her armed police officers through the massive bronze doors of main entrance of the British Museum and into the Great Court.

Inspector Sands was a brave woman who had faced the worst criminals in England. Her officers were brave men and women too, but that night their bravery was tested to the limit.

'Death or glory!' thundered King Bones and he waved his sword above his head.

'Death or glory!' roared his warriors in answer and they charged the police lines.

'Fire!' roared Inspector Sands and fifty machineguns spat bullets in the dark.

King Bones was a fearless leader in death and life, and his warriors had fought many battles against fell beasts and men. But that night their bravery was tested to the limit. Welshmen with spears they could fight. Axe-wielding Viking berserkers held no fear for them. But machine guns were too much. Again and again the warriors threw themselves at the police. And again and again the bullets knocked them back.

Firework explosions of molten metal lit the Great Court as bullets smashed through the skeletons' armour. Ancient bones splintered into dust. And still the warriors charged.

The police were down to their last bullets. Another charge and their machine guns would be useless.

'Release the dogs!' yelled Inspector Sands. It was her last hope. The barking Alsatians strained against their leads, dragging their police handlers forwards in the eagerness to join the fight.

The king saw the end. 'Retreat!' he ordered, bellowing to be heard above the deafening clamour of battle. Only then did his warriors fall back, carrying their comrades who were too splintered to walk unaided.

The skeleton army was defeated. They had lost the battle. But the war went on.

King Bones mounted his stallion and addressed his warriors.

'Do not be down hearted,' he called to them. 'While there are warriors alive or dead, your courage will never be forgotten. Songs will be sung to honour your bravery!'

Audrey began to cry. She was drowning in the sadness of the warriors. Danny held back his tears. He had cried enough today.

'Go my friends,' said King Bones. 'I will hold our enemies back, whilst you escape.'

His warriors did not waver. 'Never!' they shouted. He was their king and they would not leave him. 'Death or glory!'

'I command you!' said the king. 'My stupidity took you from your families once. I will not fail you again.'

Broken as they were, the skeleton warriors refused to leave their king. So the king told them a lie.

'On my stallion I can outrun our enemies and lead them away. On foot you will only slow me down.' The king's voice cracked as he said the words.

Dry tears ran down the brave warriors' cheekbones and splashed onto the floor forming moonlit puddles. It was the king's last wish and they must do as he commanded. The warriors locked their splintered shields to make a wall and retreated in fighting order, helping their shattered friends and leaving none behind. Except their king and they knew they would never see him again.

King Bones turned his horse towards his enemies. The police lines were advancing slowly. Beams of light from the torches strapped to their machine guns pierced the dark. The fierce dogs barked and strained against their leads.

King Bones patted the flank of his horse. 'Will you carry me a final time?'

The stallion stamped a hoof in answer and whinnied and bobbed his head. The horse was bred for war and he was brave as any huscarl.

Peeking beneath the warriors' retreating wall of shields, Danny watched the king.

He's not coming, thought Danny.

Danny wriggled under the wall and ran to the king's side. Audrey followed.

'You have to escape!' pleaded Danny.

The king shook his head.

'You have to!' begged Audrey.

The king looked away.

'You have to!' demanded the queen. 'You silly old fool! You've got my head and my dress and I want them back.'

Chapter 33

THE FINAL CHARGE

'TAKE US WITH you,' said Danny. 'The police won't shoot at children.'

'And I know the Museum,' said Audrey. 'I can show you the way out.'

King Bones took their hands and lifted the children onto his horse.

A beam of light found them in the dark. Instantly, another forty-nine converged on the king. Danny and Audrey had to shield their eyes from the blinding glare.

The king dug his spurs into his horse's ribs and the stallion bounded forwards.

'Hold your fire!' ordered Inspector Sands.

The police lowered their guns and ducked and the horse leapt high above their heads.

'Go right!' shouted Audrey and King Bones galloped the horse into the Assyrian exhibition. The king was steering with his knees, holding the queen's head under his chin, the reins in his teeth, his sword with his right hand and he was hugging the children tight with his left arm to stop them falling.

They raced past statues of man-headed winged-bulls *borrowed* by British explorers from ancient palaces in Iraq. They charged through the hall of Egyptian statuary, filled with gods and pharaohs *borrowed* from tombs and temples from Cairo to Luxor.

The police were in hot pursuit, kneeling to fire carefully aimed shots that missed and shattered ancient granite. Ramses lost a finger and Nefertiti lost her pretty nose.

'Go left!' shouted Audrey. 'No! I mean right!'

Too late. The king had already turned the horse and they galloped into the hall that housed the marble statues Lord Elgin had *borrowed* from the Parthenon in Athens.

Modern Greeks accuse Lord Elgin of stealing the statues, but that's not fair. Lord Elgin paid good money for his marbles. He paid the Turks, who, back then, had conquered Greece and borrowed everything in it. So Lord Elgin was not stealing; he was receiving stolen goods.

Either way the room was a dead end.

The horse skidded on the hard floor, his iron shod hooves gouging deep cuts into the polished stone. The stallion reared on his back legs as King Bones heaved the reins with his teeth and swung his sword around his head in mighty sweeps, holding fast to the queen's head and the children.

The horse span about, but the police had reached the door and blocked their escape. Standing shoulder to shoulder the police raised their guns ready to fire.

'Halt!' ordered Inspector Sands. 'In the name of the Law!'

'Fly my beauty,' whispered King Bones and he dug his spurs between the horse's ribs. The beast sprang forward, fresh and eager for battle.

The police kept their line. Fifty marksmen took aim, looking down the sights of their black machine guns, waiting for the command to unleash death, undaunted by the mounted skeleton warrior charging towards them on his bony steed. The light of fifty torches glinted on the blade of King Bones' sword and shone through the holes blasted in his armour. The hooves of the king's horse struck bright sparks on the floor.

'Steady!' Inspector Sands raised an arm ready to give the signal. 'Make each bullet count and shoot to kill!'

A beam of light hit the terrified faces of Danny and Audrey.

'Hold your fire!' screamed Inspector Sands – she had forgotten the children – and policemen and women scattered left and right.

The horse danced between the cops and through the door. But again the way was blocked by a marble statue of a naked goddess. The statue was a gift to the museum from an English duke, who had bought it for pennies from starving Italian peasants who had looted it from the grave of a Roman general. Which was sort of fair because the Roman general had stolen it from some ancient Greeks after he had stormed their city, burned it to the ground and sold the surviving Greeks to works as slaves in the mines. Which was sort of fair because the first ancient Greeks had stolen the statue from some other ancient Greeks after they stormed their enemy's city, burnt it to the ground and sold the survivors to work as slaves. Which was sort of fair because this second lot of ancient Greeks had used barbarian slaves to quarry the marble and the Greeks had treated their slaves abominably.

So everyone got what they deserved, more or less, except the barbarian slaves died miserably in their chains. Or maybe not. Because, by an amazing coincidence, the barbarians were Germans and one day descendants of the same German tribes would conquer England, live in Greezy, invade London and break the statue.

The horse checked its stride and leapt, flying high above the marble goddess. Until a trailing hoof clipped her cheek and snapped the statue's head clean off.

They were back in the Great Court.

'Up the stairs!' cried Audrey and King Bones steered the horse to the foot of the staircase.

The stallion galloped on without a pause, his hooves fighting for grip on the slippery steps. Armed police raced up the stairs behind them.

'Stop!' demanded Inspector Sands.

'Don't you dare!' warned Queen Bones, in case her husband waived.

'This is your last chance!' shouted the inspector raising her own machine gun and taking aim at King Bones' neck a vertebra below his skull. Inspector Sands was a skilled marks-woman who had never missed her target. Her hands did not quaver. It was her last bullet, but single shot would end the fight. Her finger tightened on the trigger and...

'E*** OFF!' shouted the queen.

It was a swear word no living person had heard for almost a thousand years, not since the Normans beheaded the last Anglo Saxon who knew it. It did not matter, though, because the *E-word* was so colossally rude everyone understood exactly what it meant.

Inspector Sand's hand shook and she fired her bullet into the floor. The other police dropped their machine guns, which clattered down the stairs, sending wild shots ricocheting around the Great Court. King Bones dropped his wife's head in horror (Danny caught it one-handed by her lower jaw). Even the horse stumbled.

Inspector Sands recovered quickest.

'Get up!' she screamed.

Not soon enough. The stallion had regained its lead and the police were left far behind. Inspector Sands could only watch as the horse galloped over the glass bridge and disappeared.

'Everyone on me!' cried Inspector Sands and the police officers collected their guns and clustered around their leader smirking and wishing they had the courage to call their boss rude names.

Inspector Sands could not care less. 'Pull yourselves together or I'll have you broken from the force.' Her fury froze their smirks. 'Have you forgotten you're supposed to be professionals?'

The police officers rapidly remembered.

Inspector Sands had a map of the museum and she sent teams of armed police in different directions to seal every escape. The sound of heavy boots echoed throughout the British Museum as the officers ran to take their positions.

Inspector Sands watched her black-clothed officers do what she commanded. 'I've got them!' she snarled in triumph.

Chapter 34

BURIED ALIVE AND DEAD

KING BONES GALLOPED across the glass bridge into the room of Egyptian Antiquities. The king knew the way without Audrey's directions - past the mummies, down the marble staircase and out through the back door of the British Museum to rendezvous with his army in Russell Square.

But it was too late. Already there were torches at the bottom of the staircase. The police had beaten them to the back door. The king turned his horse to try another route. That way was blocked as well. The police were crossing the bridge, their black boots banging on the glass. There was no escape.

The king looked about. Here was as good a place as any and he jumped from his horse.

'I'll make my last stand here,' he said and he rolled his shoulders and touched his toes, to loosen his joints.

The queen was silent. She did not protest when the king took her head from Danny and tied it by her golden hair to his belt. There was a fierce pride in her eyes. Queen Bones was the daughter and granddaughter and great granddaughter of warrior kings. There was no shame in this defeat. King Bones had done all he could and she would share his fate, whatever that might be.

The torches were in the next room. The king raised the

sword above his head. Death awaited the first enemy to find him.

Danny knew exactly what to do. Every lesson he had learned from his parents, every experience good and bad, every sorrow and triumph, had prepared him for now. He knew the future that awaited him if he was caught and he did not hesitate.

Danny slipped from the horse's back and stepped in front of King Bones.

'Put down your sword.'

The king wavered. Danny was only a boy, but he spoke with the authority of someone who knows when they are right.

Audrey jumped from the horse and joined Danny, standing between the king's sword and the police.

'It's over.' Danny's voice was calm. 'You've helped your army to escape. You've paid your debt for drowning them in the river. Killing innocent people will stain your honour. The police are only doing their job.'

The king marvelled at the children's courage.

'I will do as you command, Danny Bouygues and Audrey de la Tour,' he said and sheathed his sword.

Patiently, the king, the queen's head and Audrey and Danny stood side-by-side ready to meet their fate, whatever that might be.

Audrey took Danny's hand in hers and squeezed. Danny glanced at his friend. She had never looked more beautiful. Although there were tears in her eyes, she was smiling an encouraging sort of smile.

A noise startled them.

Tap-tap-tap! Someone was knocking on a glass display case. From the inside! It was a mummy, swathed in dirty linen bandages.

'I think she's saying something,' said Danny. He had prepared himself for defeat. Now hope was returning. 'But I can't hear what. The glass is too thick.'

Danny pointed to his ear and shook his head and hoped the mummy would understand.

The mummy did and she tapped a bandaged hand on a huge sarcophagus painted with jackals and falcon-headed gods, and mimed climbing inside.

'Of course!' hissed Danny. 'She's saying we can hide in the sarcophagus!'

Danny patted his pockets, searching for the skeleton key to unlock the display case...

...and remembered seeing the skeleton key fall from his hand and slide under Aunty Ratbag's fridge.

Audrey remembered too. She grabbed King Bones' left hand and snapped off his other little finger.

She threw the finger to Danny. 'Try this!'

The police torches were getting closer. The first beam entered the room.

Danny kissed the finger. Be quick, he prayed. The finger bones glowed softly, then, in a whizzing blur that was too fast to see, changed into a small key. Danny fitted the key into the lock and the glass door opened.

'In here,' urged the mummy and she lifted the children into her sarcophagus and jumped in beside them.

It was a tight squeeze. Danny and Audrey were at the bottom, lying nose-to-nose with the corpse of a mummified princess who had been dead for five thousand years. She smelled like an old vacuum cleaner.

'Thank you,' whispered Audrey.

'Don't mention it,' purred the mummy. She spoke immaculate English, with a exotic Middle Eastern accent. 'Now hush or they'll find us.'

The police searched the room, shining their torches left and right. They were so close their breath misted the glass of the display case. They looked into the sarcophagus, and all they saw was a jumble of old bones. The king's horse had collapsed itself on top of them, hiding the others below.

Inspector Sands arrived and her officers stood to attention. 'Where are they?'

A police sergeant, with a face like a boxer, shrugged. 'We don't know, sir,' he muttered. The sergeant kept his eyes straight ahead, not daring to look Inspector Sands in the face. 'We followed them in here, sir, but they've vanished clean away.'

Inspector Sands stamped. 'Damn and blast!' she cursed.

In the sarcophagus the children lay still and listened.

I recognise that voice, thought Danny and he imagined the shame if the same policewoman who had arrested his parents arrested him too. The newspapers would love it. He could see the headlines. The Sun's would say: *'Boy Bouygues Bungles BM Burglary.'* And The Daily Mail's front page would read: *'Half-foreign child follows French mother into a life of crime.'*

'Thieves don't vanish into thin air,' snarled Inspector Sands. 'When you've searched this room lock the doors. Then search the next room and lock those doors too. We'll go through the museum millimetre by millimetre until we catch those crooks. If they escape, I'll…! I'll…? I'll E*** the lot of you!'

Chapter 35

THE GREAT ESCAPE

THE POLICE FINISHED searching the Egyptian Mummies' room and left, sealing the door behind them.

As soon as the police had gone, King Bones clambered out and began to put his horse back together. The mummy lifted the children out of her sarcophagus and they watched King Bones' mounting frustration.

'How did you learn to speak English?' asked Audrey, as King Bones fitted the horse's rear right leg into its front left shoulder. Audrey wanted to tell the king that he had made a mistake, but she knew she had better not. The king was already cursing and swearing.

The queen sighed in exasperation. He'll never change, she thought.

'The English language didn't exist when you were alive,' said Audrey, loudly, trying to mask the king's dreadful language. They were in this adventure together and the king's swearing was showing the whole team up.

The mummy understood. She had been married too and men have behaved exactly the same since time began, from Cairo to Camden Town.

'I've been listening to parties of school children and visitors for so long, eventually I learnt the language,' the mummy explained. 'Of course the Rosetta Stone helped.'

Audrey told Danny that the Rosetta Stone was a slab of dark grey rock that the British stole from the French who had stolen it from the Egyptians. Although, at the time it was made, lots of Egyptians were Greeks. The Rosetta Stone was kept in the British Museum.

'It's engraved with hieroglyphs with a translation into Greek,' said the mummy. 'I found a Greek-to-English phrase book in the Museum's lost property office. After that, learning English was easy-peasy. I'm fluent in French too. And Spanish and Italian. And German. Some people say German's an ugly language, but I disagree. It's got a marvellous rhythm and some fabulous words. Like *strassenbahnhaltestelle*. It means *tram stop* in English. Which do you prefer? Boring *tram stop* or *strassenbahnhaltestelle*?'

'I'm studying Chinese now,' the mummy continued, without waiting for an answer to her question. She was a talkative sort of mummy. 'We get a lot of Chinese tourists in the British Museum these days. And Russians. I'm starting Russian next. You have to do something to pass the time!'

'Do you mind being taken from Egypt and put on display?' asked Danny.

King Bones was having a terrible time with the horse's ribs. There were 36 of them and they all looked exactly the same. The queen had started giving her husband advice, which was making King Bones even crosser. The poor horse looked sad and foolish, with his head attached to his bum, his tail protruding from his forehead like a drooping unicorn's horn and his legs fixed back to front.

'Not really,' said the mummy. 'It's better than being locked in a stuffy tomb in the middle of the desert. Air conditioning is the best invention ever. And to tell the truth, I rather like being admired.'

The King fitted the 36th rib in place and put the head the right way around and in the correct position, switched the legs and moved the tail. It was time to leave. They thanked the mummy and Danny and Audrey kissed her bandaged cheek. Audrey was used to dead people now and touching them did not seem strange any more.

The mummy put a bandaged hand to her face where Audrey had kissed her. It was years since she had been treated as a human being rather than an object of curiosity. The kiss had awakened long-buried memories.

'Take these,' whispered the mummy, slipping a pair of matching rings from her fingers and giving them to the children. The gold rings were decorated with dung beetles carved from rubies. 'They're a gift to remember me by.'

The children did not know what to say. The rings were beautiful and they really wanted them. But it felt like stealing.

'Don't they belong to the British Museum?' asked Danny.

'It depends on your point of view,' said the mummy. 'They were my rings long before those grave robbing archaeologists took them. They were given to me by my brother-husband, and I'm giving them to you. I don't think anyone sensible would call that stealing.'

King Bones was listening at the sealed door. The police had gone. It was safe to leave. Danny used the skeleton key to open the door, and then he returned it to the king. They mounted the stallion and the king rode to a tall window that looked out towards Russell Square. They were high up above the street, amongst the branches of the trees. Outside, the dark night was coloured blue by the flashing lights of one hundred police cars.

'Take care,' called the mummy, waving at them. 'And visit soon.'

Suddenly Audrey had a brilliant idea.

'Why don't you come with us? There's plenty of room on the horse.'

The mummy was tempted. She had been alone for so long. The other mummies really were dead. It was a common side effect of having their brains scrambled and pulled through their noses with a hook. 'Is it better than here?'

Danny looked around, at the magnificent room and the remnants of the glory of Ancient Egypt. And he thought about Greezy and the stinky pet food factories and the chimneys belching filth.

'Not better, just different,' said King Bones, because the king was blind to Greezy's present faults. For King Bones, Greezy would always be his capital city.

The mummy shook her head and stepped back into the display and waved goodbye.

'Hold on tight, everyone,' shouted King Bones, taking a firm hold on the reins. 'Yah!'

He slapped the horse's flanks and the stallion sped forward. The horse leapt at the window. The glass shattered and they flew through the air.

The horse's bones crunched when they hit the ground. Police officers dived for cover from the deadly shards of falling glass and the horse galloped amongst them, skipping nimbly, left and right and left again with frightening speed, never stumbling or stepping on a policeman's foot. The stallion's hooves drummed on the road as he charged towards Russell Square. He jumped the metal railings with a foot to spare.

The skeleton army was mounted and ready to go. There was no time to explain.

'Onwards,' commanded the king. 'We ride to Greezy!' and they galloped along Upper Woburn Place, across the Euston Road and into Euston Station.

Chapter 36

TOGETHER FOREVER

NO ONE SAW the column of weary warriors pass by the dog food factory and dismount by the old church. No one watched them carry their precious bundles into the church and return empty handed. And no one watched the warriors waiting outside with growing impatience for their wives to get dressed.

The church clock struck five o'clock, then six.

The horses pawed the earth. They had to be underground before dawn and it was getting early.

'What's taking them so long?' complained King Bones, who was beginning to wonder if rescuing the queen had been a dreadful mistake. He had forgotten how long she took to get ready.

'You'd have thought after fourteen centuries she might have learned to hurry up,' he muttered.

The warriors nodded in agreement.

The more things change, the more they stay the same, thought Danny, without realizing it was exactly the sort of thing Mr Bouygues might have said.

'I'll see what's keeping them,' said Audrey and she ran down the stairs and waded through the mist into the secret chamber.

Chaos reigned. The warriors' wives were wailing and

pulling their hair. Their dresses had been ripped to shreds by police bullets.

'Lock us in again!' they demanded. 'And throw away the key!'

Audrey was tempted to do what they asked. Instead she gave them a piece of her mind. 'You ungrateful, selfish women. Your husbands risked their deaths to rescue your clothes and jewellery and you're complaining about a few holes?'

The women were unmoved, so Audrey tried a different tactic.

'Anyway your clothes are hopelessly out of fashion,' said Audrey, in her matter-of-fact voice. 'Nobody's worn dresses like that since the Norman Conquest. They're so 1066. If you like, you could give me some treasure and I can go shopping for you. You could wear a new dress every day.'

The women stopped wailing. It was a tempting offer.

One more push should do it, thought Audrey.

'And modern underwear is so much nicer than your scratchy old things. I can buy you silk knickers, if you like.'

Audrey knew that silk was a luxury few Anglo Saxons could afford. Even the queen wore woollen knickers. They itched horribly. In the summer her knickers gave the queen heat rash. Or, at least, the memory of heat rash.

'Perhaps we should go,' said one of the ladies-in-waiting. 'After all, the men have tried so hard.'

The others agreed solemnly and they quickly put on their torn clothes.

Then Audrey noticed that Queen Bones was missing. Audrey found her at the back of the secret room. The queen was already dressed. She wore her tattered clothes with pride because she knew how the holes had been made. She was only late because she was having trouble fixing her skull onto her neck. Audrey clicked it into place.

'Thank you,' said the queen.

Danny was standing at the top of the stairs when he heard their footsteps. He raced outside.

'They're coming!' he shouted.

The horses whinnied with excitement.

The women were unprepared for their reception. When their husbands saw them they ran forward to embrace their wives. And when the wives beheld their bullet-shattered husbands they were ashamed and proud. Ashamed for their silly vanity. And proud because they loved and were loved, without condition, with all the love that two people can share.

Queen Bones came last. Her clothes were the most tattered of all and she looked magnificent. The queen offered her hand to the king and he took it. As their hands touched a blue light swirled around them and for a moment they were whole again. Real people of skin and muscle. The queen had buttercup hair and cornflower eyes. King Bones' red hair reached to his shoulders and his bulging belly stretched his armour. They kissed and the light faded. Once again they were skeletons.

'Forever,' said the queen.

'Forever,' echoed the king.

Chapter 37

SORRY IS THE HARDEST WORD

IT WAS THE most difficult thing Danny had ever done. He stood in front of the gravedigger's hut searching for the words to say what he felt.

At Danny's lowest moment, when everyone in the world despised him, the gravedigger had offered Danny his friendship. It was another of Mr Bouygues' sayings: a friend in need is a friend indeed.

Danny had a new best friend, but the gravedigger was the first. And Danny had insulted him.

The gravedigger had been right about everything. Almost. Stealing was not a slippery slope. It was the greatest fairground ride ever invented. When it went wrong it was thrilling. When it went right, the rush made Danny feel more alive than he thought was possible.

Every day since their arrest, Danny had racked his brain trying to understand why his parents had stolen the Crown Jewels. Now he understood. It was for the adventure.

Danny had lied to the police. He had always known about the box under his bed and what was in it. And who had put it there. It was his dad. Danny had caught Mr Bouygues sliding it under the bed. Mr Bouygues told Danny that the box contained a surprise birthday present for Mrs Bouygues. He had made Danny promise not to look.

Danny broke his promise. He opened the box and found the Crown Jewels. He had laid them out on his bed and put Queen Elizabeth's Crown on his head. He had shone a torch through the Koh-i-Noor and made a thousand rainbows dance on his bedroom wall.

The next morning, when his parents were at work, Danny had searched their room and found the clothes his father had worn for the robbery and an identical set in his mother's wardrobe.

Danny could have told the truth and saved himself. Instead, he lied to the police to protect his parents.

It had not worked. They were in prison and he had been sent to Greezy to live with Aunty Ratbag. And now he was busy making the same mistakes they had made.

Not any more, swore Danny. My life of crime ends here.

Before Danny could knock, the gravedigger opened the door of his hut. And before Danny could say sorry the gravedigger's gruff face broke into the broadest smile.

'You've had a big night,' chuckled the gravedigger. He knew that Danny was sorry and sometimes, between friends, knowing is enough and the words are not needed.

In the background Danny heard the gravedigger's radio. The break-in at the British Museum was the top story.

'I'm making hot chocolate,' said the gravedigger. 'Do you want some?'

Chapter 38

THE SILENT WATCHER

NO ONE HAD seen the column of weary warriors pass the dog food factory and dismount at the old church.

No one? Not quite.

One person was watching from the shadows, hiding behind a horsebox filled with exhausted seaside donkeys. The person was a man. Unless it was a woman. It was impossible to say for sure.

The first light of the new dawn revealed a green uniform with reflective patches on the shoulders and a green peaked cap pulled down low over his – or her – face. It was the uniform of a traffic warden.

Not wanting to be seen, the traffic warden stepped back into the deeper shadows, awkwardly, as if something was wrong with one of his – or her – legs.

The traffic warden was keeping a close watch on the strange proceedings. But he - or she - had no interest in King Bones and his skeleton army or the queen or their treasures.

The traffic warden was only interested in Danny Bouygues and what might be in Danny's pocket.

Chris Hallatt Wells lives in North London with Lucille and their children, Spencer and Lily. King Bones is his first published novel.

And if you like trolls and witches...

MAXIM'S ALL NIGHT DINER
Mikka Haugaard

Annabel is doing research on witches in London – there are plenty of them if you just know where to look and not just in London, but in New York too, hiding in Grand Central Station. In fact, everywhere – beneath the dull surface of the everyday – lurks the world of magic. And no one knows more about magic than Maxim the troll but can he be trusted? Can you trust anyone when magic has been let loose?

'Haugaard writes with wit, flair and invention.'
The Independent

Or a fantasy involving other worlds....

DYLAN AND THE DEADLY DIMENSION
Mark Bardwell

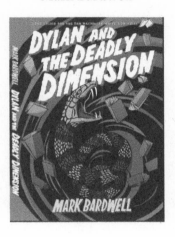

Dylan never knew a bookshop could be sinister until he met Mr Ebenezer. But ever since that snake in the bathroom, strange things have been happening. Creatures from other realities have taken to appearing suddenly. RollovkarghjicznilegoghVylpop- hyngh or Rollo for short, a strange creature from another reality is one of them. Rollo is his friend and Dylan needs a friend. Or is he?

'An exciting story full of humour, twists and turns, weird dimensions and characters.'
Primary Times

'Fast-paced adventure.'
Kirkus Reviews